HERITAGE FULFILLED

The Heritage of Three Strands
Not Easily Broken

Caroline's Heritage Series

Book Three:
Heritage Fulfilled

Gaile Thulson

Cup of Water Publishing

HERITAGE FULFILLED
Copyright © 2022 by Gaile Thulson

All Rights Reserved.
No part of this book may be reproduced, scanned, or distributed in any printed or electronic form without permission.

All people, places, and events of this book are entirely fictional. Any resemblance to real people, places, or events is coincidental or used for fictional purposes.
Trademarks mentioned in the text are the property of their respective owners. No endorsement or association is implied by their use.

Scriptures taken from the *Holy Bible, New International Version®, NIV®*. Copyright © 1973, 1978, 1984, 2011 by Biblica, Inc.™ Used by permission of Zondervan. All rights reserved worldwide. www.zondervan.com The "NIV" and "New International Version" are trademarks registered in the United States Patent and Trademark Office by Biblica, Inc.™

Cover design © 2022 by Cup of Water Publishing, LLC

ISBN 978-0-9973279-6-0 (Hardcover)
ISBN 978-0-9973279-7-7 (Paperback)
ISBN 978-0-9973279-8-4 (eBook)

To Jesus, the Great Shepherd and Healer,
with much gratitude

Caroline's Heritage Series

Book One: Heritage Restored
Book Two: Heritage Reclaimed
Book Three: Heritage Fulfilled

The boundary lines have fallen for me in pleasant places; surely I have a delightful inheritance.

Psalm 16:6

Heritage Fulfilled

The Heritage of Three Strands
Not Easily Broken

CHAPTER ONE

"Surprise!"

Caroline was surprised. It was Saturday, two weeks and one day before her birthday, and Peter had suggested they stop by his parents' house for lunch to talk to them about wedding plans. There was a lot to do, in spite of the amazing progress they had made. On his parents' recommendation, she and Peter had planned their honeymoon and made the reservations so that they had the luxury of choosing the locations and the actual rooms before it was too late. She and Peter had reserved Caroline's church for the ceremony, along with the attached hall for the reception. Everyone was working hard to make the wedding flow as smoothly as possible. Working with Peter's mom, they had just managed to send out the invitations last week; so thanks to Claire, a long and much more involved process than Caroline had anticipated was finally finished.

She hadn't expected Peter's parents to plan a birthday party just for her, especially two weeks early, and especially with the wedding coming so soon, during spring break. She looked around with a smile on her face. Peter's family was there, of course, but his parents had also taken the trouble to invite former and current members of the Christian leadership team at the university as well as friends from her church. As a result, there was quite a crowd, and they were all people with whom she enjoyed spending time.

"Mia! Jeff! How are you?"

"Doing great!" Jeff replied. Mia was all smiles, and Caroline knew from recent conversations with Mia that she and Jeff were seriously dating. Now that they had graduated and chosen another university to work on their master's degrees, at least they were attending the same university which meant that they were still able to consistently spend time together. Caroline was happy for them even though she missed them.

"I hear good things about the leadership team," Jeff continued. "I was just talking to Josh and it sounds like you guys have some interesting events planned."

"We still miss you, Jeff," Caroline assured him, "but Josh is doing a great job. Now we have Peter to join us, too! Jeff and Mia, this is Peter, our new official faculty sponsor."

"And your fiancé! We are so happy to meet you!" Mia exclaimed with her usual exuberance. Caroline knew she meant it: Mia had been praying for the right timing for Caroline and Peter. She needed to thank Mia for her prayers!

Only God could have worked out the timing with Peter's job and all of the events leading up to his marriage proposal in the gazebo that he had built in her yard at Christmas!

"So, did your bridesmaid dress arrive?" Caroline asked.

"Yes! It's beautiful! I knew it would be," Mia answered.

"Have you tried it on? Does it need any adjustments?"

"The fit is perfect."

"Are you sure?"

"Absolutely."

"Okay. Let me know if you think it needs any tweaking. I could help." Caroline offered.

"You are not to worry! It's perfect the way it is."

"May I have your attention?" Peter's father Brett had to nearly shout over the good time everyone was already having. "Burgers will be served as soon as we pray for them!" He waited for the room to quiet. "We want to welcome you and thank you for coming. Thank you for being special friends to our future daughter-in-law."

"Not just friends! We're fans!" shouted Lyndsey, a member of the Christian leadership team at the university. Lyndsey and Drew began the clapping and whistling that grew to include everyone in the room.

"As are we!" stated Peter's father, still smiling when the noise had died down. "So, thank you for sharing this very special twenty-first birthday party with Caroline. We wanted to make it memorable!"

Brett's prayer was brief but thankful, and he and Grandpa John were soon bringing in platters filled to overflowing. By the time everyone was enjoying burgers stacked with their favorite garnishes and condiments, Caroline and Peter had been able to greet many in the crowd. There were a few people Peter hadn't met before, and she loved the way he so quickly found common ground with each person he met. She was convinced that no one could help but love him as much as she did.

"Jo, I'm sure you had a lot to do with this!" Caroline whispered when she found herself standing next to Peter's sister, though she had no idea where Jo had found the time in addition to her seminary studies.

"Oh, something to do with it," grinned Jo.

"I'm not surprised at that, but I'm so surprised by all of this! I had no idea!"

"Then it's a success! You really had no idea?"

"No idea! I was totally surprised! I can't believe you contacted all of these people. How did you do it?"

"Oh, I have my ways! Josh was a great help with the leadership team, past and present. The people from Grandma and Grandpa's church were easy to contact. Of course, we had to include the Larsons and Dr. Calton and his wife. Grandma Martha helped with the planning. Grandpa John insisted on bringing the burgers and all the fixings. I think everyone is having fun."

"Everyone seems to be having a wonderful time. Thank you, Jo. I'm so glad you could come home for the weekend. You're amazing, as always!"

"It's fun, isn't it! Everyone brought cards for you to look at later. We'll save family gifts for tomorrow after church. Do you mind if we celebrate so early? We're all invited to Grandma and Grandpa's tomorrow. That leaves you some time to get ready for Peter taking you out on the special day."

Caroline laughed, "Ha! You must know something I don't know."

"Could be," Jo said smugly.

"Well, thanks for the warning. What kind of dress will I need? Or will I need something more casual?"

"Oh, no. You're going to need something very fancy!"

"That's just great. I don't think I have time to shop for a fancy new dress!"

"Well, quoting someone I know, 'Fortunately, elegance is simple.' Wasn't that what you said? I'm sure you'll come up with something very nice, like you always do. Maybe next weekend I would have time to go with you. We can try your favorite shop!"

"Sounds like fun, but with the wedding costs and my schedule I may have to wear something I already have."

"Let's talk after we look at our schedules," suggested Jo.

"Okay, but really, I have the dress I wore for our first date."

"I don't know if I've seen it. You'll have to show me."

Drew and Lyndsey, already done with their hamburgers, rushed over to hug Caroline and wish her a happy birthday.

"How's that canoe?" Drew asked, referring to the vintage canoe he and Lyndsey had selflessly restored for Caroline. "Still safe and snug in the boathouse?"

"Oh, yes!" Caroline replied. "But this summer I can't wait to get it out. Peter will be able to handle it, thankfully. I still can't believe you two did all of that work. It's beautiful!"

"Yeah. Too bad Peter wasn't around last summer. We would have put him to work!" Lyndsey kidded.

"Who would have put me to work?" Peter asked, joining them.

"We would have! We could have used another pair of hands on that canoe!" Drew chimed in.

"Oh! The canoe! It *is* beautiful!"

"That's what I keep telling them," Caroline laughed.

"I look forward to paddling Caroline around the lake. You did an incredible job on it!" Peter said.

Lyndsey interrupted with her usual teasing directed at Drew. "Beginner's luck!" she stated, causing laughter. They all knew both she and Drew had grown up around boats and had restored enough of them to become experts.

"I enjoyed working on it," Caroline said. "What little you two would let me do, that is. It was a lot of fun."

"It was fun," Lyndsey agreed. "And you served us the

best lunches we've ever had working on a boat."

"It was the least I could do," Caroline said, giving her another hug. "I still think I should pay you, at least for the materials!"

"No way," Drew stated. "Just seeing it restored to its original glory is worth it."

"Come by and take it out anytime," Caroline offered.

"We'll take you up on that as long as you serve us lunch!" Lyndsey joked.

"Ha! It's a deal!" Caroline agreed. Drew and Lyndsey had made the long drive from their hometown several times over the previous summer just to give her vintage wood canoe a makeover. It would be fun to have them come back when she and Peter could entertain them.

"The dress is stunning, Caroline. It just came yesterday." Lyndsey informed her.

"Have you had a chance to try it on?"

"Are you kidding? I couldn't wait to try it on. It's the nicest bridesmaid dress I've ever seen. I love the fabric and the soft blue is perfect. Blue is one of my favorite colors, maybe my most favorite!"

"That's a good color for you. I'm sure it looks great!" Caroline affirmed. "How's the fit? I can help if it needs adjusting."

"Everything is perfect. It's just a little long but that's easy to fix."

"Oh, I'd love to hem it for you!" Caroline exclaimed.

"I have to confess that I'm not much of a seamstress, but my mom is all over that hem. I think she's working on it as we speak!"

"Does she like to sew?"

"Yes. She used to make me the cutest little skirts and dresses when I was little."

"How sweet!"

"The dresses, yes! Me, not so much. I've always been such a tomboy. The only time she could get me to wear them was on Sundays to church."

Caroline laughed, "I know what you mean."

"I'd much rather be out on the lake fishing with my dad than anything else."

Caroline smiled mischievously, knowing there was another person Lyndsey enjoyed being with.

"What?" questioned Lyndsey.

"Oh, nothing!" Caroline said with exaggerated innocence. "But there is someone else you spend time with on the lakes."

"I can't imagine what you mean," Lyndsey said, copying Caroline's innocence before breaking into a grin.

"Caroline, Lyndsey! The dress came!" Gabbie said, rushing over to them. "I love it! It's beautiful!"

Caroline wondered if her bridesmaids liked the dresses as much as they claimed. It was certainly part of their role to claim to love them. Didn't every bridesmaid bravely put on whatever the bride requested whether sophisticated, simple, or frilly? Didn't every bridesmaid forever after have a dress they could never wear anywhere else? Jo had a plan to shorten her maid of honor dress after the wedding so maybe the bridesmaids could do the same. It was Jo who had helped her find the dresses. Since they both thought the dresses were tasteful, hopefully the bridesmaids really did like them. But she was getting nervous with all this talk about the dresses. No one had asked about her wedding gown and she didn't want to admit that she had made exactly zero progress in that direction. She was thankful when the conversation turned in a different direction. She didn't necessarily want advice or help. It seemed like such a personal decision and she wanted to make the choice on her own. She was the one who had to be happy with the way she looked. This week she would focus on her dress. It had to be out there somewhere!

Much later, she and Peter stood at the door thanking the guests as they left. Each of these people meant so much to Caroline. As she spoke to them individually, she was struck by the things each had contributed to her life and Christian growth. Turning away, she hid the tears welling in her eyes as God reminded her of just how faithfully he had answered her desperate and angry cry for people who would care about her. It had been her first prayer in her grandparents' home, if you could call it a prayer! Now, with gratitude and humility, she thanked the Lord silently in her heart for hearing her ignorant and ungrateful demand. While we were still sinners, Christ died for us. *How true! Thank you, Jesus!*

Later, after Peter had dropped her off at home, Caroline spent the rest of the day focusing on completing class assignments before turning to her senior project. Yes, she was getting married at the young age of 21, very unexpectedly and to her own surprise, but she was also scheduled to graduate in May and she knew with the wedding and a brief honeymoon happening during their spring break there would be no time to pull coursework together at the last minute. She would have to stay on top of it. She had found that reserving Sundays for church and family yielded its own rewards, and with all of this additional celebrating going on it looked like she was going to be extra busy.

It was late by the time she reached a good stopping point on her project but thinking about the next day made her smile. She loved Peter's grandparents who lived next door to her and she loved spending time with them. It was Peter's grandmother who had introduced them, sending Peter over with her homemade blackberry pie to help Caroline acquire the computer she had needed when she first arrived. Looking back on her decision to come and claim the house her grandparents had left her, she was amazed at her own bravery. Or naive audacity! It had been hard, but she was so glad she had made that decision. God had brought her so far since then!

The next day, glancing around the church sanctuary, Caroline reflected on how church had become such a blessing, especially now with Peter sitting beside her! It was his grandparents' church, the church his mother had attended while growing up. It had become Caroline's church and from now on would be Peter's as well. Though he had grown up attending a church across town, closer to his parents' home, he had often visited with his grandparents and was quite happy with the new arrangement. Caroline's minister would be the one to marry them and they would be meeting with him for the required premarital counseling sessions before the wedding. He greeted Caroline and Peter warmly after the service.

"Are we still on for Thursday?" he asked.

"Absolutely!" Peter replied.

"I know you two are busy. Have you had the opportunity to begin on any of the covenant readings I gave you?"

"I'm almost finished," Caroline replied.

"Me too," Peter added.

"Wow! That's great! If we can discuss what you've learned on Thursday, we'll be ready to move ahead."

"I've learned so much, I don't know where to begin!" Caroline exclaimed. "But I am taking notes."

"Wonderful!"

"I've learned a lot, too, Peter admitted. "I thought I already understood the idea of covenant and had some good background on it, but I've been surprised at the depth behind the concept. It means so much more than I knew."

"Great! And remember not to discuss it between yourselves. I want to hear from each of you Thursday! Seven-thirty," Pastor Sanders reminded them.

Caroline and Peter had driven to church separately that morning since Peter was living at his parents' house until the wedding. Caroline drove home and parked her MG convertible in the garage, thankful that the snow was not deep enough to make driving difficult. Peter parked on the street a moment later. They were soon busy helping Grandma Martha set the table and prepare the salad. Sunday dinner, as lunch was called, would be ready by the time Jo and her parents arrived. Grandma already had the birthday banner in place and Caroline smiled thinking back to her last birthday when she hadn't bothered to tell anyone about her birthday until Jo and Grandma Martha had discovered they had missed it. Grandma Martha had insisted on immediately hanging the birthday banner in place and putting a cake in the oven. Life had been simple then, but lonely, Caroline realized. *Thank you, Jesus!* She was grateful for how different life was now. What a difference a year made!

Dinner was followed by fudgy, triple-layer birthday cake and candles. She did not reveal her birthday wish, but it seemed natural that her wish turned into a prayer to her Heavenly Father for his blessings on their marriage. It was

God, after all, who was the giver of good gifts. He was the only one with power to actually grant a "wish."

Grandma Martha brought out a sturdy basket decorated with a colorful bow and presented it to Caroline.

"From all of us!" she explained.

It was filled with smaller wrapped packages that she was obviously supposed to unwrap, so she began with what turned out to be fancy pruning shears. A gardening basket! The next package contained gardening gloves which were followed by several pairs of short stakes attached by twine.

"They're just the length of your gardening boxes," Peter informed her.

"Oh, wonderful! My rows will be extra straight now," Caroline stated with satisfaction. Last spring she had hastily put together some temporary string guides to help her plant her seeds in straight rows. It had worked, but these would be much easier to use and reuse.

There was a package containing several seed packets and the largest package contained a heavy-duty, high quality trowel and fork set.

"Very nice!" Caroline exclaimed. "My trowel separated itself from its handle. I never did figure out a fix for that. Thank you! Thank you, everyone!"

"There's an envelope in the bottom," Jo said.

Caroline thought Jo looked very pleased about something. She opened the birthday card which was signed by everyone in Peter's family, and out fell a gift card to her favorite clothing store. Jo, of course, knew it was her favorite, but the amount on the card was way more than Jo could have given.

"Jo!" exclaimed Caroline.

"From everyone," Jo assured her.

"Wow! Thank you! Thank you, everyone!"

"Now will you go shopping with me later this week?" grinned Jo.

"Yes! Wow! Thank you for such a wonderful birthday!" She was amazed that they had all been so generous when they were already contributing so much to the wedding. Her own focus had been entirely on the wedding, but they had chosen to make her birthday special as well.

Later, Peter carried the basket home for her. They wandered from room to room talking about things that needed doing in the house and ended up in her grandfather's study, discussing the computer upgrades each of them really needed. Plenty of upgrades could be fun, but with a limited budget they were focused on what they could afford and on what would actually make life easier and improve their work.

"We'll have to figure out how to fit all of your computer stuff in here," Caroline stated. "I want you to use Grandfather's desk. I guess I'll need another desk. Maybe something a little more feminine but still large. Would there be room to put another desk here?"

"I don't want to intrude on your space," Peter said. "You need your own study area. Maybe I could use another room."

"But I want you to use Grandfather's study."

"Is there a room you would like to have as your own?" Peter asked. "What about the library? I know you love that room."

"I hadn't thought about it. I like that idea but I want you to be able to use the library, too, and it's so beautiful as it is. I don't want to mess it up."

"What if we got you a really nice desk and office storage units to match the library? I could still use the library to sit and read but it could be your special place. There's so much storage here in your grandfather's office. I'm afraid I'll have all of the advantage of hiding unsightly messes in here. All of my books can go in here. All of my teaching files. All of the household accounts. If you only need space to have your classwork and thesis, maybe we could make it presentable. Let's go see if it's feasible to make a beautiful workspace for you somewhere else!"

Caroline's spirits always lifted when she entered the library. Was it the natural lighting that flooded the room? It was a beautiful room and she enjoyed playing the grand piano when she had time, but she suddenly realized she hadn't spent much time in what was probably her favorite room. She had decided from the beginning that she couldn't carry her course work and textbooks to her grandmother's beautiful third story retreat every day, so she had used her grandfather's study as the obvious choice.

"This room is a lot more feminine," observed Peter.

He was right.

"I'm not the neatest person when I'm in the middle of a project. I hate to leave a mess where everyone could see it," Caroline said. "I guess I could close the doors if I needed to."

"What if we put a desk in this corner at the back of the house, something really nice that would look right in this room? With matching office furniture behind it and down this wall, you would have enough storage to keep things out of sight. And this corner isn't really visible from the other rooms."

"Maybe. That sounds expensive."

"I do have a salary. It's not a large one, but …"

"I just haven't gotten used to the idea of having real income," Caroline stated.

"Well, you'll get used to it," Peter encouraged. "It's *our* income. We share everything from now on. You insist on putting my name on the house with yours after the wedding, so I insist on a joint bank account. Everything I have, little as it is, is yours."

Caroline had no reply. It was the right thing for both of them to do. It was right to share everything God had given them.

"Nothing yours or mine, only *ours* for the rest of our

lives," Peter summarized, pulling her into his arms and gently kissing her.

CHAPTER TWO

Caroline loved his profile. She could draw it from memory, she was certain, but sometime when Peter wasn't looking she would try it when she could sneak a few peeks before he figured out what she was doing. Being engaged to Peter was... like finding a place to belong in the world. First, God had given her a home in this world, a literal house provided for her by her grandparents. Then God had revealed his love for her, saved her, and promised her an eternal heavenly home with him through faith in Jesus, his Son. Now, he was giving her a husband who did his best to walk with God every day. Her husband-to-be had grown up in a family that relied on God and they lived grateful lives before God, but she was sure Peter could hardly appreciate his Christian heritage as much as she did on his behalf. His family had become hers, another answer to the lonely cry of her heart for people who truly cared for her.

How bleak the world had looked when she thought Peter cared for someone else! But God had been faithful, even in her despair, even in her decision to go away if that were so. Through that heart-wrenching time, she had learned that she could take her faith in Christ anywhere and that Christ himself would go with her. She knew with a deep certainty that her spiritual heritage belonged to her and was her own, her own personal faith in God, rooted eternally. Her relationship with Jesus was not dependent on Peter, nor on his sister Jo who had helped Caroline find Jesus. No matter what the future held, no matter where she went, she knew God loved her and would take care of her in this life and in the life to come. God had given her that assurance. And in the end, God had given her Peter.

She had tried to explain it all to Peter with inadequate words, and she knew he understood, but she doubted that he could ever really understand the depths of her profound gratitude to Jesus. She had gone from being an orphan with no one and nothing to her name, to a place of belonging, first of all, in God's family and, secondly, in Peter's family. She had even found her place in her own family's history and she was at peace with that history. *God is good.*

Discovering her grandmother's walk with God had helped her along her path toward belief in God and in His goodness. What was that verse? *Without faith it is impossible to please God, because anyone who comes to him must believe that he exists and that he rewards those who earnestly seek him.* Faith is an act, an action taken that assumes God's existence, and not just his existence, but his goodness as well. God is! And if we seek him, he promises to be found. When she'd first come to her grandparents' home she had known nothing about God, but God had changed that! Peter was reading her grandmother's journals now. He said he wanted to understand Caroline's heritage. He said that he wanted to know everything about her. It had been hard at first to let him into a world that was so private, to give him the journals and have him know all of the weaknesses and ungodly details of her mother's family, but she wanted him to see how faithful God had been and how God had answered her grandmother's prayers to save each of them in the end. Caroline looked forward to seeing her grandmother, her grandfather, her uncle, and her mother someday in heaven. *God is good.*

༶

The next day, Caroline stood in the doorway of the master bedroom that had been her grandparents'. She had looked on it with awe for so many reasons. When she had first arrived as a nineteen year old she had certainly not had any interest in moving into it. It was too luxurious. It hadn't seemed right to disturb her grandparents' things, as though usurping their place in the house they had left to her. But all of that was different now that it would be Peter's home as well. After they were married, they would share this room as husband and wife.

Now that Peter had finished his doctorate, it was nice to have him here in town instead of so far away, and seeing him on campus every day as "Professor Berkhardt" left her shaking her head at God's goodness. Only God could have accomplished that. Now, with the blessing of the university administration, their engagement was known and accepted. They were waiting until after the wedding to live together, an idea that followers of Jesus understood but that others found strange. Why wait? Because there was priceless spiritual meaning in marriage, spiritual meaning that they valued. They were doing their best to explain to those who were curious that marriage had meaning beyond the obvious. They had both been celibate and would remain so until their marriage.

Peter was bringing pizza later this evening. They were going to start clearing out the master suite so that it could be painted before the wedding. This moment, before Peter came, was her only opportunity to privately and reverently process her grandparents' belongings and the passing of the baton. The house that had witnessed her mother's childhood would become the home where she and Peter would raise their family. Peter's participation in making it theirs was important to her, but she had never even really looked at the contents of her grandparents' room and she needed to do that alone. She wanted some private time to feel close to her grandmother.

She sat on the side of the bed and began to fill a box with the items from her grandfather's bedside table, smiling all the while because of the memory of finding the keys to the MG there. When she had needed a car, God had definitely provided. It was working on the MG that had given her time with Peter when he was still living so far away. *God is good.*

And here were all of her grandfather's other keys. She left the two large keyrings out on top to give to Peter. She recognized a few keys to the house and garage and they would have fun trying to figure out what all the rest of the keys unlocked. Maybe Peter would know what some of this stuff was that Grandfather had left in his drawers. She walked around to her grandmother's side and began transferring the contents of her bedside table to another box. She had decided against throwing away their things even though they were without personal meaning to her. She just wasn't quite ready to dispose of things had been important to her grandmother. There were cards from people she didn't know, scraps of paper in the precious handwriting of her grandmother, an old transistor radio, a flashlight, and a notepad of paper labeled "To Do" that made her smile. It was always a surprise and a confirmation to find ways in which she was like her grandmother. She left a few of the things in the drawers that she supposed she would find useful, smiling again at the memory of discovering the envelope here with her name on it in her grandmother's flowing script. Inside had been the key that opened the door to her grandmother's third floor retreat. It was in her grandmother's third floor study that Caroline had found the diaries containing the joys and sorrows of her grandmother's married life. It was there Caroline had discovered what it meant to be a Christian. A real Christian. It was in the journals that she had read about her grandmother's faith in Christ. She had read her grandmother's prayers for the salvation of her husband and children. She had read her grandmother's willingness to lay everything in this life down for the blessings of eternity with Jesus. And Grandmother had seen God's goodness in circumstances no one would normally call good.

Caroline believed, as had her grandmother, that the best and most expensive things of this world could never compare with knowing Jesus. For most of his life, Caroline's grandfather had made the mistake of thinking it was the other way around. He had not valued the most valuable things. He had neither valued a relationship with God, nor the relationships in his family. He had not even cared for the friendship of godly people like Peter's grandparents next door. It wasn't until he gave his life to Jesus that he began to value the unseen things of God above his own possessions. It was reassuring to know that Peter held those same deep convictions and priorities: to him, God was first, and she wouldn't have it any other way.

Her phone broke into her thoughts: it was evidently time

to deal with the wedding florist. She needed to check flowers off of her To Do list, and hopefully it wouldn't take long. Peter had let her take the lead in choosing flowers. He wanted her to be happy with them and he was helping with the cost. They both liked the samples Caroline had decided on at the florist's.

"Yes, calla lilies," Caroline stated, running down the stairs to retrieve her detailed list. "White roses and white calla lilies for my bouquet with the pearl insets, just like you showed us on Saturday.

"Just the white callas with white ribbon and pearls for each bridesmaid to carry. Four of those. Then, for the pew ends, white roses and white calla lilies with ferns tied with white ribbon. Those go on the inside end of the first three pews on each side. So, a total of six of those for the pews."

"Okay, great! Let's move on to the men's flowers," urged the young lady, as Caroline referred to the notes on the paper in front of her. The florist on the phone seemed a little too eager.

"Three white roses with a fern for the groom's boutonniere," Caroline obliged, "and one white rose and fern for the four groomsmen. Two more of the same boutonnieres for the father and grandfather of the groom, and, uh, two more grandfather boutonnieres." They had decided to include the Larsons as though they were real grandparents. "That's seven boutonnieres plus the groom's. Oh, and one tiny one for the little ring bearer. Just a rose bud and small fern for

25

him. Then we need four more boutonnieres for the ushers."

"Okay, corsages," the florist prompted. "Your corsage will detach from your bouquet, so you can do the traditional tossing of your bouquet."

"Right. That's good. Let's see. Three white rose buds and small ferns to be wired to the basket for the flower girl. We'd like white rose petals for her to scatter. How much do you recommend? Okay, that sounds good.

"Then, three grandmother corsages." She silently reviewed the list of people: Grandma Larson, Grandma Martha, and Peter's grandmother on his father's side, whom she'd met briefly a year ago. That first Christmas had included an unexpectedly large crowd of Peter's father's relatives. This Christmas had been more intimate and she had begun to feel like part of the family. "One mother of the groom corsage…"

"You don't have flowers for the bride's family," the florist on the phone interrupted. Caroline studied her list again.

Peter's Grandpa John would be walking her up the aisle, though Grandpa Larson, and Dr. Calton seemed to feel some responsibility for bringing Peter and Caroline together. Each of them meant so much to her. She didn't want to hurt their feelings. Had she included Dr. Calton's boutonniere in the count? Dr. Calton and his wife would be welcoming people at the guest book. Caroline looked forward to getting to know

Peter's grandmother on the Berkhardt side, but she was a widow, so no boutonniere would be needed.

"Uh, no parent-of-the-bride flowers," Caroline stated firmly. "I need one more boutonniere for the guest book.

"Two large standing candelabra will need bouquets of white roses, callas, and ferns. And white ribbon."

She reviewed the totals with the florist and hung up the phone feeling relieved. *I can check that one off the list.* Peter and his parents were taking care of the groomsmen and their tuxedos, so she didn't have to worry about them. She reassured herself again that the bridesmaid dresses were simple and elegant. Her gift to each of them was an inexpensive necklace that would look perfect with their dresses. The girls would look lovely and the white and powder blue colors of the wedding would be perfect in the light blue church sanctuary.

But what am I going to wear?

So far, in spite of hours spent, her search for the wedding dress that she envisioned had been in vain. Was that the problem? Vanity? She seriously wanted to look perfect for Peter. She smiled, thinking of the last time she had dared to ask God for help to find the right dress! *Thank you, God, for helping me find that amazing dress for our first date. I really need your help now, Lord.*

In her heart, she'd been talking to the Lord about her wedding dress for weeks now, but every dress that seemed to call her name was way beyond her means. Her petite size seemed difficult to fit as well. She had dared to look online at the kind of dress she dreamed of, but common sense would not allow her to spend that kind of money, especially on a dress she couldn't try on first. She was hesitant to order something that might not fit as it should. She didn't want to have to keep returning dresses that didn't work. She had also inevitably come to the conclusion that she simply didn't have the kind of money to buy the best dress at a shop in town where it could be fitted. *So what do I do now?*

She really didn't have time to sew her own wedding dress, and she didn't want to ask anyone she knew to sew it for her. That was too much to ask of anyone, and there really wasn't time to design and fit something that might or might not end up looking professional. She had priced fabrics and it didn't seem any less expensive than buying a dress readymade. In the end, it was her responsibility to come up with a wedding gown. She would just have to keep looking. God would provide, somehow. Her thoughts were interrupted by her phone.

"Hi, Grandma Larson!" She did have a wealth of grandparents, in spite of not having any real ones of her own! The Larsons weren't even related to Peter, but they had claimed the privilege of "adopting" Caroline from the very beginning. *Oh, no! We need another corsage for Mrs. Calton at the guest book! I'm going to have to talk to that florist again.*

"Hello, Caroline. I know you probably already have your

wedding dress, but Sam and I would like to cover the cost of your dress. We want to contribute to your wedding in some meaningful way."

"Oh, Grandma Millie, I couldn't let you do that!" *I'm sure she has no idea what they cost today, at least the ones I'm interested in. How could I possibly ask for such a sum? Would they be willing to contribute part of the cost? That doesn't seem like a very appropriate solution, but I can't ask them to spend what I want to spend.*

"Do you have your dress already?"

"No, I'm still looking. That's so sweet of you, but I couldn't... "

"Have you considered using your grandmother's dress? I know girls these days want things more modern, but her dress was so beautiful. I think the style would look very nice on you. Sam and I talked it over, and we would like to cover the cost of cutting down your grandmother's gown if you decide to use it. I know it would require alteration, but I know this wonderful tailor who would do an excellent job. I've given her my business for many years and she's never disappointed me."

Grandmother Emily's dress?

"I do love Grandmother Emily's dress," Caroline said, trying to process what Millie Larson was saying. "I've seen it in their wedding photos. You're right: it would look very nice, but I haven't seen it here. I..."

"I believe it's in your grandmother's closet, up on the shelf in an archive box. Or in the attic. She had it cleaned and put away to preserve it. That's where it used to be, anyway. Maybe it's not there anymore, but I can't imagine Emily parting with it. It meant so much to her."

Caroline realized she'd been holding a picture of her grandmother's gown in her head as the unattainable ideal she hoped to find somewhere out there in a wedding shop. Could it possibly be here, in the house?

"I'm going to go look! Can I call you back?"

"Okay. You don't have to use it, but I thought it would look so lovely on you."

"Thank you, Millie! I'll call you back later if I find it, okay?"

Caroline was already dashing up the stairs. She swung open the door to her grandparents' lavish room again and stood, taking stock, like she did every time now when she entered. It still seemed to belong to them, not to her, but a fresh coat of paint in this particular room would be the first step to making the house a true home to share with Peter.

She walked across the room and raised all of the blinds, letting light fill the space. Dust danced in the sunbeams. She had occasionally dusted and vacuumed in her grandparents' room, but until now, she had wanted it to remain as they had left it. She may not have felt grown up enough to claim it for herself when she'd arrived, but it was time for a change.

They planned to decide on the paint color that evening when Peter came. She had been gathering paint samples and hoped to move ahead quickly. The romantically long drapes would come down for a simpler, more modern look. She wanted a lighter, brighter room.

Caroline crossed the room to her grandmother's closet. It was entirely possible that Grandmother Emily's wedding dress was still here. *Please let it be here, Lord, if it would be a good solution.*

Within a few minutes, she was standing in front of the full-length mirror, clad in white, holding in various parts of the oversized gown. Grandmother had been taller and slightly larger, but the proportions were similar to hers. She admired the softly gleaming fabric, evaluating the overall effect. The sophisticated lines could easily be altered to fit her. It was going to be perfect! She would work with the tailor to make sure it was a flattering fit. It seemed sad to cut it down, but it was just waiting to be put to good use! Without a doubt, Grandmother Emily would be pleased to have her granddaughter wear her wedding gown. It would definitely require a professional to do the fitting and adjusting. *If I had all the time in the world, I might attempt it myself, but what a gift from the Lord and from the Larsons! A professional tailor is just what I need! I have to call Millie.*

"Grandmother Millie? Guess what! I'm wearing my grandmother's dress!"

"You found it?"

"Yes! Just where you said it would be. It's perfect! I love the fabric and the tiny pearls are so beautifully sewn."

"Oh, I'm so glad, Caroline!"

"It will require altering, and I think I *will* need the help of a professional tailor."

"Well, I will have my tailor give you a call so you can set up an appointment. I'll tell her it needs to be done immediately. But don't you worry! She's the best there is. I'm so happy you found it. I hope Emily knows!"

"Me too!"

"And you're not to worry about the cost one bit. Sam and I will be so pleased to know we made it possible for you to wear Emily's wedding dress. Besides, altering it won't come close to the expense of a new one. Isn't God good?"

"He is! And so are you and Sam. Thank you so much!"

There were tears in Caroline's eyes when she ended the conversation. If she hadn't been so busy, she might have thought to ask someone about her grandmother's wedding gown before, but then she may not have known from the beginning that it was perfectly and exactly what she needed, or that there was a trusted professional available to alter it for her! God was so good!

Peter arrived joyously with a huge pizza, boxes of his books to add to Caroline's grandfather's study, and a surprise.

"Close your eyes," he instructed before sliding the engagement ring onto her finger.

"Oh! The rings came! How wonderful! I love it!" Caroline exclaimed holding her diamond up to flash in the light. "How are the others?"

"They are just as they are supposed to be, inscriptions and all. See?"

"Oh, I love them! Let's see the inscriptions… "

"To Peter. And to Caroline," he read. "Plus the date, just like our instructions."

"It looks nice. I like the script. Did they spell everything right?"

"They did, so you can stop worrying about the rings now."

"I'm not worrying. I just want them to be right. Are all of the dates right?"

"Yes, so no more worrying. They're going back in my pocket until the wedding." Peter said rather smugly. "Let's eat! I'm starved."

Caroline had the kitchen table already set, so they sat down and Peter captured Caroline's hand before praying God's blessing on the food and on their evening. They were both happy to dig into the multi-topping pizza along with the iceberg salad with lots of fresh veggies that Caroline had fixed.

"I talked to the florist," Caroline informed Peter.

"Oh, did you get the flowers ordered?"

"Yes, but I have to call her back and add a corsage for Mrs. C."

"So you ordered boutonnieres for all of our old gents?"

"Yes, I did," Caroline replied, laughing.

"You have no idea how popular you are with that crowd. You should have seen them after church Sunday. When I happened on them, they were dredging up all the hilarious wedding stories they could come up with. They're determined to be part of the fun, and I can't say that I blame them!"

"Well, they're all wonderful! So it will just make all the more fun for everyone."

"As long as they behave themselves. They'll all want to kiss you, you know, after the wedding."

"No they won't!" She was scandalized by the thought. She would outmaneuver them with a preemptive peck on the cheek and stay out of their clutches.

"I'm just saying, you have a pretty ardent fan club."

"Oh, that's silly!" She changed the subject. "By the way, I have my wedding gown!" She couldn't help but grin excitedly.

"What? What's it like? Do I get to see it?"

"No! Of course not," she said, grinning again.

Not wanting Peter to get too curious about the wedding dress, she steered him toward other topics having to do with the new look they wanted the master bedroom to have.

"What can we do to update the bathroom? The tile isn't bad, really. It's in good shape."

"What if we have some new bathroom fixtures installed?" Peter suggested.

"But we might need to wait to work on the bathroom until after the wedding. I don't think there's time for that. If we can just get the bedroom redone so we can settle in, I'll be happy."

"Jo has volunteered to help us paint."

"Great! That will help," Caroline said with a smile.

They ate and cleaned up the kitchen in a rather short time and headed up the stairs.

"Let's order the shades so they get here in time. We settled on white shades, right, to go with the white trim? It won't matter so much what color we choose for the walls," Caroline reminded Peter.

"Sounds good to me."

They measured carefully and made a list of what they needed before placing the order. Caroline was glad that Peter was willing to help. Two people agreeing on the dimensions meant they were less likely to make a mistake.

"Now we can focus on the paint color," she said with relief.

"This color is a little dark," Peter said, referring to the color already on the walls.

"I really want something very light and neutral," Caroline said, holding up some samples. "It will seem so much fresher in here."

"That one looks good," Peter said, pointing.

"I like that. Or maybe this one? Here's a good white for the trim. This one looks good with the white."

So many choices! It was more difficult to make a decision than Caroline had expected, but eventually they agreed on the paint color. It was going to be so pretty! She couldn't wait to see the room all fresh and clean and updated.

CHAPTER THREE

Peter was driving and had picked her up, so Caroline suddenly found herself with time to reflect. She didn't know what to expect at their first marriage counseling session, scheduled to take place at Pastor Clay's house. She was surprised to find that she was a little nervous but reminded herself how friendly he and his wife Julie were and tried not to worry. She and Peter were greeted warmly and offered dessert. They were soon sitting comfortably around the Sanders' kitchen table.

"I always include Julie in my marriage counseling sessions. I'm also willing to give either of you a private session if you request it, but I find having Julie here helps keep a balance and openness to our chats. Is that all right with you, Peter? Caroline?"

"Sure!" Peter agreed.

"That's fine." Caroline was surprised and happy to have the presence of another woman, a woman she respected and trusted.

"To begin, we'd like to hear how you came to know Christ. It's always a treat to hear how God brings people into his family. Peter, why don't you begin?"

"Sure. I'm happy to share. I was six years old when I asked Jesus to forgive my sins and come into my life and heart. My mother sought me out one day and asked if I would like to. She tells me I was very unhappy and out of sorts that particular day. I don't remember that part," Peter said with a grin. "I do remember the actual event. Very clearly. Mom made sure I knew the importance of what I was doing. She checked my understanding of the gospel and prayed the sinner's prayer with me: I asked Jesus to forgive my sins, for him to come in and make his home in me. After we had prayed, I felt clean. Like a new person. Jesus has been with me every day since. He's the center, the root, my reason for existing. He's my life."

Pastor Clay was smiling. "We know you had the privilege of growing up in a Christian home where you were taught about Jesus and became familiar with God's Word as a child. But, Caroline, I know your story is different from Peter's because I've heard your testimony and I've had the privilege of baptizing you recently. Would you share how you came to know Jesus as your Savior?"

"Yes. You know I was raised in foster homes because my parents died when I was young. God protected me from my own parents' lifestyle of addiction and brought me back to my grandparents' home to find Jesus through my grandmother's journals and her faith. Peter's sister, Jo, is the one who sought me out and helped me pray to receive Jesus when I was needy and ready. I will always be grateful. Jesus has brought such joy and peace to me. I know I have a lot to learn, but spending time in God's Word every day has become so important to me. I hope to continue to grow as a Christian every day of my life, but I don't think I'll ever catch up to Peter and Jo."

"I wouldn't look at it quite like that," Pastor Clay said with a twinkle in his eye. "There are wonderful blessings about growing up in a Christian home, something you'll be able to pass on to your own children now, but there is a freshness, an affirming truth about the Gospel when adults respond to the good news of Jesus. Both are valid ways of coming to Christ. Both affirm the offer from God that all who call upon him with childlike faith will be saved. Julie grew up in a Christian home, but I came to know the Lord in college through a Christian organization that was active on campus. I know both of you are involved in sharing your faith on campus, and that really resonates with my heart. But, right now, I want to continue to explore the great mystery of marriage with you."

"Oh, good! I'm going to need help with that!" joked Peter.

"Don't we all!" Pastor Clay commented, giving his wife's

hand a gentle squeeze. "We're going to change gears now and discuss the readings I asked you to do before coming. So the topic was the idea of covenant. How did that go? Were you able to fit the readings into your busy schedules?"

"No problem. I found it fascinating. I actually learned a lot," Peter commented.

"How about you, Caroline?" Pastor Clay asked.

"It was life changing!" Caroline exclaimed.

"Great! Let's start with this question: How would you define covenant? What is a covenant?"

Peter politely waited for Caroline's comment first, unknowingly escalating her insecurity.

"I suppose I would begin by saying it's a very serious, binding agreement between two parties," she managed to say.

"That's a great start! Peter, can you give us some history behind it?"

"After the study you started us on, I would say it's something very important to God. He built covenant into the world he created from the very beginning, as far back as Adam and Eve. I learned from our assignment that even though the word 'covenant' wasn't used in the Biblical account until Noah came out of the ark, there are earlier examples of God initiating interventions on behalf of his sinful people."

"So, I hear you partially defining covenant as a God-initiated intervention on behalf of sinful people?"

"Originally, yes, I think that was its true definition. In ancient times, covenants in many different cultures had to be sealed with blood in some way. I guess we've lost the historical definition of covenant. In many ancient cultures it had to do with two people making an agreement that was a huge commitment to one another. I was surprised in the readings to discover that they actually took on one another's debts, one another's defense, basically one another's identity. They actually mixed their blood in some way, either by cutting themselves and holding the cuts together or, in some cultures, even by mixing a drop of blood in a cup of liquid and drinking it! They became blood brothers. I never realized the connection between the old "blood brothers" ritual and the idea of covenant!

"Some covenants were with a stronger and a weaker party, so the stronger was pledging protection to the weaker party. With God, I guess that's always been the case. Continually, through Biblical history, God took the initiative as the stronger party, offering protection and blessing even though we don't deserve it."

"Good overview!" Pastor Clay said. "There are hints of covenant in the Bible as far back as God's provision of animal skins to clothe and cover Adam and Eve's shame after they had broken God's one law, breaking their covenant with him, about not eating from the Tree of the Knowledge of Good and Evil. Their leaf coverings, made by themselves, were evidently not adequate in God's eyes.

"Then, when Cain and Abel were required to bring a sacrifice to God, it was Abel's bringing his very best in the form of the first-born animal sacrifice that was such a rebuke to Cain and his offering of 'some' of his garden produce. The taking of life, even an animal life, was a costly and serious thing in God's eyes, but it seemed to be his requirement to atone for sin in the Old Testament times. Let's look at Genesis chapter 6 now. Caroline, what did you think about the covenant God made with Noah? Could you describe it for us?"

"Well, like Peter said, it was initiated by God. His purpose was to save Noah and his family from judgment. He decided to save them, to rescue them out of the consequences of all the horrible sin that defined the world then."

"And what two different categories of animals was he to preserve?"

"Clean and unclean. More of the 'clean' ones."

"What was the difference? Do you think Noah understood the difference?"

"He did what God told him to do, so at some point he must have understood that there was a difference to God," Caroline reasoned.

"So, Peter, what did Noah do with the 'clean' birds and animals when he came out of the ark?"

"He sacrificed some of each of them to God. Meaning he

killed them and offered them on an altar to God."

"Why do you think he did that? It doesn't say that God told him to."

"Well, now that I think about it, he must have already had an understanding of what God required: the shedding of blood. God had considered him a righteous man so Noah must have retained knowledge of God's requirements and practiced them, maybe even before the flood as well."

"Good point. We know from what happened later that Noah was not perfect, but God called him righteous because he believed and obeyed God. What was God's response to Noah's righteousness?"

"First, to save him from the flood," Caroline stated, paging through her Bible. "And then in Genesis chapter 8 to decide never to curse the ground again because of sin and never to destroy all living creatures because of sin, as he had done with the flood."

"Right," Pastor Clay commented. "And in chapter 9 he blessed Noah and his family and established a covenant that he would never again use a flood to destroy all life on the earth. It became a covenant established by God with not only Noah but with all living creatures. The rainbow was the sign he gave of his intention to keep that promise. When is the next time God makes a covenant with someone?"

"Abraham," Peter responded, paging ahead to chapters 11 and 12 of Genesis.

"Yes. A covenant with Abraham's descendants, the Israelites," Pastor Clay commented. "It would take a long time to trace every example of covenant in the Old Testament of the Bible. What are some that stuck with you?"

"I thought Jacob and Laban's covenant was interesting because they agreed not to come against one another, not because of love for one another but, I think, because of their mutual love for Jacob's family, and their fear of God," Peter commented. "But, much later in history, I was really impressed by the way Joshua honored the covenant the Israelites made with the Gibeonites, even though the Gibeonites had tricked them into the agreement. They considered it a solemn oath before God, regardless. Joshua went to their defense when they were threatened, and the amazing way God honored their effort to defend the Gibeonites that's recorded in Joshua chapter 10 just about outdoes any of God's interventions on behalf of his people."

"Extending the length of a day is pretty amazing," Pastor Clay affirmed. "God thought so much of this covenant that many years later he sent three years of famine on the country of Israel because King Saul tried to destroy the Gibeonites. Second Samuel chapter 21 tells us King David had to hand over two of Saul's sons and five of his grandsons to be killed by the Gibeonites in order to make it right. We're talking about severe consequences for breaking that covenant."

"It's alarming to see how far we have gotten away from

God's laws," Peter said. "It's a good reminder for me that God is long suffering. He doesn't give us what we deserve."

"But God forgives if we ask him," Caroline said.

"Yes," said Pastor Clay, "if the request for forgiveness comes out of repentance, God's forgiveness can cover an innumerable multitude of sins. God's mercy and grace are without limit because of the forgiveness available through his Son. So, Caroline, was there a particular covenant that stood out to you?"

"I think it was Jonathan's covenant with David. Was it First Samuel it's recorded in?"

"Yes, chapter 18."

"Jonathan initiated the covenant and they exchanged clothing and weapons, committing to defend one another," Caroline continued.

"What was remarkable about that?" asked Pastor Clay.

"Jonathan was the son of the king and he basically put David on equal footing with himself, as though they were brothers."

"So, what are the pros and cons of entering into a covenant with another person?" Pastor Clay asked.

"You want to be careful about who you make a covenant with because it's for life." Peter commented. "God considers it binding and there are serious consequences for anyone breaking the covenant. It's both a pro and a con. Both parties have the assurance that the other person will consider it binding. That gives a peace of mind, a trust in the other person, because it's an agreement before God, not just a promise between two people."

"Yes, the initial decision should be a cautious one," agreed Pastor Clay.

"I suppose it could affect the rest of your life. The impact could be huge down the road," Caroline commented. "It could require more of you than you expect.

"Are there benefits as well?" Pastor Clay prodded.

"Yes," both Caroline and Peter assented without hesitation.

"Someone to have your back. Someone who is on your side," Peter continued. "Someone who has taken an oath with God as the witness has a lot of incentive for keeping that oath."

"Someone to protect you and take your side, to stick up for you and provide for your needs. Not just money needs. Someone who will support you in other ways, too," Caroline added.

"Keep those positives in mind and continue to add to them. Here is your assignment for our next meeting," Pastor Clay said, handing them each a piece of paper. "These are passages to look up about the New Covenant that God offers us through his Son. That's what we'll be talking about next time.

"But there is something else I'm asking you to do this

week. I want you to consider, individually, in prayer before God, whether you are ready to enter into the marriage covenant. I want you to drive here separately next week. If you decide you can't enter into this covenant for life, simply don't come next week. That may seem drastic, but God prefers that you don't come to that conclusion *after* the marriage. I know this week may be awkward, but it's your chance to decide if you can make that commitment to the other person. Don't worry about one another. Your job is to decide for yourself. Continue your marriage plans as needed and, please, don't discuss the actual decision with one another. I'll be praying for you both."

Peter and Caroline were serious and troubled during their leave-taking and drive home.

"I'll see you tomorrow night," Peter said, walking her to the door. "Jo's working on finishing a paper early so she can help."

"She's amazing!" Caroline said, trying to be cheerful.

Each of them were on their knees as soon as they were able, asking the Lord to guide them, asking for his will to be done. Peter couldn't help but wonder if Caroline would be there next week, and Caroline couldn't help but wonder if Peter would come.

Perhaps he would change his mind and decide she wasn't worth it. Pastor Clay had said not to worry about the other person. She would do her best to examine her own heart.

The next day, she picked up some ice cream and rushed home as soon as she could to make Peter's favorite cake. It was the only thing she could think of to show her love for him. Jo would be there to help them eat it and relieve some of the awkwardness for the evening.

Peter and Jo arrived with fish tacos and all the necessary "fixings" which they all enjoyed before starting on the painting. Peter and Caroline tried to appear normal for Jo's sake and they were soon able to put their troubled thoughts aside.

They planned to tackle the ceilings tonight and address the walls the next morning. They would have all day tomorrow since it was Saturday.

"Are we doing the bathroom?" Jo asked.

"We've decided to remodel it later this year. It's too big a job to take on right now," Caroline replied.

"Let's see if we have enough plastic drop cloths to cover up the closet fixtures and both floors," Peter said, removing the wrapping from one of the packages. "We'll need to take that picture down, Caroline."

"I tried. The funny thing is, I haven't been able to move it," Caroline explained. "I don't know how it's connected to the wall."

"Let's have a look," Peter said, confident that he could remove it.

"I've tried everything I can think of."

Peter tried lifting, shifting, and pressing with no luck. "How much do you like this painting?" he asked.

"I don't know. I thought I would move it to another room, maybe."

"We'd better research the artist so you can decide if it's worth it to damage it in the process of removing it."

"It's a safe!" joked Jo. "It's in the classic place for one."

"Ha! You could be right," Peter acknowledged. "But, even so, there has to be a way to move the picture to get at the safe, right?"

"Right."

They each took several turns at trying to move the picture, without success.

"I suppose we could put a drop cloth over it while we do the ceiling and then paint around it when we do the walls," Caroline finally conceded.

"I hate to do that but maybe we should for now," Peter said.

"It looks like the frame sticks out enough to get a small brush behind it all the way around. It will look normal and you can do the touch up when you figure it out," suggested Jo.

"Yeah, I guess so."

"That's fine with me, Peter," Caroline said. "It's held us up long enough."

"True. We have a lot to do in one evening. Okay, let's

49

figure out what we're doing. How about I begin by loosening light fixtures in the closet and the main room? If I brush under them right away, then they won't be in the way when we start to roll later."

"Caroline, I could brush the ceiling edges in the closet pretty quickly if you want to get the paint trays and rollers ready," Jo offered.

"Sounds good," Caroline replied, beginning to assemble what they would need. She found herself wishing she was the one working in the walk-in closet with Peter and tried not to resent Jo's presence. It was the first time she had ever felt that way. *Lord Jesus, help me never to resent Jo's presence. Thank you for her, Lord.* Maybe it was just as well that Jo was in there. Things seemed awkward with Peter, no matter how hard they both tried to act normally. She wished they could talk about it, but she could understand Pastor Clay's request that they not discuss it until next Thursday. What would she do if Peter didn't show up Thursday? He certainly didn't need her. He could choose any wife he wanted. Anyone would be thrilled to receive his attention. She recognized the sinking feeling she'd experienced before Christmas when she had thought he cared for someone else. But she had told the Lord then that she wanted what God knew was best. The Lord had given her a deep assurance that she would still be able to live out her new faith in Christ, regardless of what happened or where she went with her broken heart. So now, she reassured herself with the memory of the love Peter had expressed when he asked her to marry him. She couldn't go back to that dismal place inside where she had been when it seemed hopeless. She would distract herself with the painting preparations. *This is in your hands, Lord.*

Peter soon came out, and gave her a quick but quite satisfying kiss. "Before Jo comes out of there," he whispered with a twinkle in his eye. "Now, I need to figure out this light fixture," he said and proceeded to try to loosen it so he could paint beneath the base of the chandelier-type fixture. He knew Caroline liked it and he didn't want to break anything.

Jo finished the closet prep and came out to hand off her brush to Caroline. Jo would roll the closet ceiling while Caroline would begin brushing the edge of the bedroom ceiling. So, Caroline set up the ladder in a corner to begin the brushwork along the edge of the ceiling, and Peter soon began in the opposite corner, having finished with the ceiling above the light fixture. When Jo finished with the closet ceiling, she grabbed another brush and began on another side of the room. By the time they had finished rolling the main ceiling and cleaning the roller and brushes, they were unanimously ready for cake and ice cream. They were hopeful that one coat of fresh white would cover the old white and had carefully searched for any missed areas.

Peter made coffee while Caroline cut the cake and Jo topped each piece with a generous scoop of ice cream.

"Do you think he'll notice the cake?" whispered Jo, echoing Caroline's silent thoughts.

Caroline smiled. "I hope so."

"What are you two whispering about? Or does it have something to do with bridal array that I am not supposed to know about?"

"I was just wondering if you would notice that Caroline made your favorite cake for you," Jo said with a teasing smile.

"Of course I would notice!" Peter came over and cut another piece of cake, adding it to the large piece already on his plate. "See?"

Jo and Caroline laughed and shook their heads.

"I think he noticed," Jo commented.

Peter capped his actions by taking Caroline in his arms and bending her backward for an exaggeratedly romantic kiss. With an embarrassed face, Caroline struggled up for breath.

"Yep. I think he noticed!" Jo commented again.

With large smiles, they sat down to their cake and ice cream.

"I'm sorry we rode together tonight," Jo commented, looking embarrassed herself. "I should leave and give you two some time alone."

"No worries," Peter assured her. "I need to go, too. Besides, we'll all be back tomorrow." He leaned toward

Caroline, saying, "By the way, you made my favorite cake!" He continued making comments like, "Wow! This is really great cake! What kind is it?"

Jo looked at Caroline and asked, "Are you sure you want to marry this guy?" Jo, being totally sure of their love for one another, remained blissfully unaware of the inner twinge of fear she had caused each of them.

Later, on the way home, Peter contemplated the question Jo had jokingly asked. Caroline certainly didn't need him. She was brilliant and beautiful. Why was she contented with him? Maybe he had pressured her into a quick wedding when she might not be ready. She was young. She was athletic. There were so many young, handsome athletes on campus she could choose. Why would she want to marry a professor like him?

That night neither Peter nor Caroline slept well even after praying and committing the outcome to Jesus.

They were all tired by Saturday afternoon, but the walls were covered with two coats of clean new paint. Jo and Caroline had to delay their shopping trip for another week, which Caroline didn't mind. Peter and Caroline would work on the trim through the week as time allowed.

"It looks so nice!" Jo exclaimed. "It's much brighter."

"Yes, I thing I'm going to like it," Caroline agreed. "What do you think, Peter?"

"I like it. I think the color is good,"

It was a long week and the awkwardness persisted. Peter

stopped bringing over his belongings as he had been doing each time he came and Caroline tried not to notice, tried not to wonder at his motive. The necessary wedding plans continued but much of the joy was missing. Caroline hadn't realized how much she had enjoyed making even the most stressful and pressing decisions that had to be made. She prayed continually. What if all these plans had to be cancelled? Jo was able to take an afternoon off to come home and insisted on taking her shopping for that perfect new dress, but it was difficult for Caroline to enjoy the outing even when they found the dress. By Wednesday, she had answered her anxieties with the assurance that she knew her mind about it, regardless of what Peter's decision would be. On Thursday evening she arrived early at Clay and Julie's house and was the first to appear. She took shelter in the Sanders' home and in their presence, gladly accepting their offer to pray with her while they waited. Caroline tried to hold back the tears brought on by their loving prayers on behalf of Peter and Caroline.

When the doorbell rang, Caroline dried her tears, holding her breath to listen for any clue as to whether it was Peter or a lost pizza delivery driver.

Pastor Clay grasped Peter's hand and drew the eager young man inside. "You've had the advantage of seeing Caroline's car. I think there's someone in here who is going to be very happy to see you."

He ushered Peter into the room where Caroline stood waiting for him and closed the door to give them a few moments alone. What they said to one another at that time stayed with them all of their married lives. They were committed to one another and they would reference this conversation anytime they doubted that fact.

A knock on the door preceded Pastor Clay and Julie's entrance. "We come bearing gifts to celebrate with you," Julie said with a grin. "I think you said you hadn't decided on a cake yet, so we have a few choices for you to taste. These are samples from three different cake places that I've noticed have great track records. We get to eat a lot of wedding cake! It's one of the perks of doing premarital counseling," she explained with another grin. "I chose three different flavors, based on the kinds Caroline said she was considering."

"Oh! That is so thoughtful of you!" Caroline was excited to have the expert help Julie was offering them.

"So, how was your week?" Pastor Clay innocently asked once they each had their plate of samples.

"Terrible!" Peter exclaimed.

"Horrible!" Caroline said simultaneously.

"You realize that's a good sign, don't you?" he asked.

"I see what you mean, but it seems a bit of an unusual approach to premarital counseling. Have you ever been accused of breaking up couples?" Peter asked, truly curious.

"I'm afraid so. I always follow up with individual and

joint sessions if I can talk them into it. Sometimes couples work through it and proceed with the marriage. Sometimes not. I know it seems extreme, but our culture has lost the true meaning of covenant. Most people who get married today don't even know they're entering into a lifelong covenant in God's eyes. As a young pastor, I sought the Lord's help about marriage counseling and became convinced that at the root of every long-term marriage was a commitment by both parties to a life of faithfulness, no matter what. So, Peter, did you learn anything about yourself while you were going through this terrible week?"

"Phew!" Peter let out a breath slowly. "I guess I did as I look back on it. I learned how much I love Caroline and how devastated I would be if we weren't able to go ahead with the wedding. I learned, again, that God is faithful and brings even greater joy when we are able to surrender to him and ask for what is truly best. Not that he always gives us what we want, but in this case, I sure am grateful that he did. It's a good reminder to always look at our marriage in that light and to continue to be grateful."

"How about you, Caroline?"

"I went through a similar time of anxiety just before we got engaged, when I thought Peter cared for someone else. It was terrible, and I had to come to terms with my faith in Jesus being able to carry me through no matter what the outcome." Seeing Peter's troubled face, she squeezed his hand reassuringly. "I did learn that my love for Peter was enduring enough to make me willing to enter into a covenant for life.

"I had learned so much about what a covenant really is from our readings and discussion," she continued. "This week I had the opportunity to think about what that means in a Christian marriage. It's so different from the way our society looks at marriage these days. Taking it as something that can be undone down the road causes so much pain to so many people. I can see now why it's so hurtful. It's the breaking apart of one person, not two, and God has built in emotional and practical consequences that are impossible to avoid. It's important to make that kind of commitment only if you have found a person who knows and loves Jesus."

"I would say you both know what you're signing up for and we should proceed with joy." Pastor Clay's gentle, knowing smile reassured them. "So, during this terrible week you also completed some readings about the New Covenant. I hope it was of some comfort to you. How is God's covenant through Jesus the same or different from all the previous covenants he established?"

Peter commented, "The way you stated that makes me realize that it's God's final covenant. It's his final commitment and it encompasses all people and all people groups for all time. It's like it says in the book of Hebrews. In the past, God spoke in many different ways, through many different people; 'but in these last days he has spoken to us by his Son.' Jesus died for all people and nothing can undo what he did. For those who believe and accept his sacrifice on their behalf, nothing can take us out of his hand now or ever."

Caroline nodded. "I was amazed, though, when I read about how the New Covenant was foretold by God in his dealings way back with Abraham. After waiting so long for God to fulfill his promise of giving Abraham a son, then God made this seemingly totally unreasonable demand that he go and offer that son as a sacrifice to God. I am astounded when I think of Abraham's faith and obedience. God had provided Isaac, so if God demanded Isaac to be the lamb for sacrifice, then Abraham believed God would raise him up and give him back to his father so that God could fulfill the promises he had made about Isaac. That's incredible faith, but because of Abraham's obedience, God was able to stop him and give him the message that God himself would provide a substitute sacrifice for Isaac, just as he intended to give his own son as a substitute sacrifice for all of us."

"I can see that made a deep impression on you," Pastor Clay said.

"The readings on it were so amazing to me. I'd heard in church about Abraham's willingness to sacrifice Isaac but I didn't really understand how significant that kind of trust in God really is."

"Can either of you think of any other aspects of Christ's sacrifice that agree with the general idea of covenant?"

"I don't think I ever completely understood why Jesus said in the book of John that we have to eat his flesh and drink his blood to have eternal life," Peter said. "He explains that he is the true bread from heaven, sent from the father in heaven like the manna. The manna gave the Israelites life and receiving Jesus gives us life, but you can see why many of his disciples turned away and stopped following him. It is hard to understand and does seem offensive. I never let it turn me away but I didn't understand it. I knew it was part of his sacrifice, giving his blood like the innocent, perfect lambs, but I didn't connect it to the idea of covenant in terms of the two parties. I think the clue is John 6:56 where he says that whoever does so remains in him and he in them.

"Learning that the giving of blood was part of the covenant, of becoming so aligned that you basically become one person instead of two, allowed me to see that was part of Christ's commitment when he took on human form and died for us. He took on our sins when he was sinless. And it was part of God's promise to *us*, part of becoming a new person in Christ. Our destiny, as followers of Christ in covenant with God, is to become like Christ."

"It ties into what he said at the last supper, doesn't it," Julie said thoughtfully.

"Take and eat this bread. It is my body. This cup is my

blood of the covenant," Pastor Clay paraphrased Matthew. "Perhaps he was actually saying it represents both the sacrifice and the oneness we can now experience with Christ when we believe and accept him and come under the New Covenant.

"Well, I know you are busy people and it's getting late," continued Pastor Clay. "I want to thank you for your thoughtful approach, both of you. Perhaps we should end the evening with prayer."

Caroline tried to store his prayer in her memory. It summarized the commitment they had each made to Jesus and the commitment Peter and Caroline were making to one another.

"You have no homework this week except to enjoy the wedding preparations and to look forward to building a home together after the ceremony. Next week we'll take a new direction but you don't have to worry about it now. We have two sessions left, but this week is for celebrating!"

Peter and Caroline grinned at one another. This, they could do.

CHAPTER FOUR

The next evening, Peter showed up at Caroline's house wearing a cheap lei and a Hawaiian shirt.

"What?" Caroline laughed when she opened the door.

"I've got barbeque, and I've got a lei for you, and I thought we'd paint to Hawaiian steel guitar music. Are you ready to celebrate?"

Caroline stepped aside to let him in. "Okay." She laughed as she followed him to the kitchen where he began taking containers out of the bag he carried. "Where did you find all of this?" she asked, amazed.

"Anything for you, my dear. Let's eat!" He whipped out his phone and started some Hawaiian music. "Allow me," he said, gallantly slipping a lei over her head and ending by kissing her.

The barbeque was delicious and Peter kept her laughing the entire time. Fresh pineapple, and a large number of side dishes with dubious connections to Hawaii gave her more laughs.

"Let's clean up this mess and get busy!" Peter finally commented, rubbing his stomach with a satisfied smile on his face. "Have you ever been to Hawaii?"

"No. Have you?" Caroline replied.

"Once when I was a kid. Maybe we can go someday."

"Maybe." Caroline had never even considered the possibility. What other potential experiences were ahead of them? She had never thought that far ahead. Life suddenly widened into interesting ideas! *I'd better reign in my imagination!* "I found this office furniture online that might work in the library."

"Let's see." They looked it up and discussed the sizes of the pieces available. "We'll have to take the measuring tape in there to see what will work," Peter concluded.

It wasn't long before they realized that the dimensions offered just wouldn't work very well in the room or give Caroline what she needed.

"Mom and Dad had some cabinets built not long ago."

"I know they were very happy with the results, but isn't that an expensive way to go? Custom built?" Caroline asked with a frown.

"Let me talk to the guys who did it. I've got the dimensions of the area. Let me see how much they would want. They may be able to match the library cabinets and build them in so they fit the space."

"That sounds so expensive."

"We'll see. In the meantime, we can share your grandfather's study."

"Okay. Do you mind helping me go through all of

Grandfather's paper files and records? I've done some of that but there is a lot I haven't even looked at."

They spent the rest of the evening and all day Saturday shredding outdated income tax records and receipts, trying to clear entire file drawers for their own use. They were committed to looking at each piece of paper before it went in the shredder, so there were entire files they saved to look at later.

"Look! Isn't this a receipt for a safe?" Caroline asked, going through a file on the building of the house. "We should probably save everything in this file."

"It does look as though a safe was installed by this company. Would you like me to research it for you?"

"That would be great. I don't know anything about safes!"

"I don't know much, but maybe Dad can help. Do you mind if I tell him about the picture?"

"No, that's fine. Maybe he can help us figure it out."

"I guess we shouldn't tell very many other people. If we ever figure it out, we might want to use it ourselves!"

"Ha!" Caroline laughed, trying to imagine owning anything so valuable that she would keep it in a safe. *Maybe important papers about the house and property or school or something?*

Peter lingered in the entryway saying goodbye that night. "I'll see you at church in the morning. And don't forget I'm picking you up at six tomorrow night for a very special birthday dinner."

"I won't forget," Caroline assured him. She was so glad Jo had insisted on a new dress. They had found a beautiful one that fit like a glove and complemented her coloring. She was confident she would be well dressed no matter where he was taking her.

She was still surprised on Sunday evening when they rounded the last curve in the secluded driveway lined with evergreen trees and their grand destination was revealed. The château-like building was stately and full of the mystique of steeply-roofed towers and intriguing windows. Caroline found the whole experience magical. They were shown to a lovely table beside one of the many fireplaces. The white cloth, candle light, and sparkling glass made an elegant picture but Peter could only think of the picture Caroline made sitting before him with one of the red roses he had brought her that she had pinned to her dress.

Caroline hardly felt like herself, and when Peter told her again how beautiful she was, she came very near to believing it. She kept her wits about her by reminding herself not to begin to expect treatment like this as the norm. This was a special occasion. So, she reasoned, she would allow herself to enjoy it, every moment of it. It was wonderful to be here with Peter.

They enjoyed the shrimp appetizer and the crisp salads with fragrant warm rolls and real butter. Caroline was already feeling full when the main courses arrived, but the Veal Oscar she'd ordered was extraordinary. She had never had veal before. She loved asparagus. She loved Béarnaise sauce and had, in fact, never tasted lobster. She was not disappointed. She could tell Peter enjoyed his *filet de bœuf*. By the time she had finished, she couldn't possibly have eaten a bite of dessert so they lingered over coffee and tea.

"I have something for you," Peter said, drawing a small box from his pocket. "Happy birthday!"

"Peter!" She unwrapped the small package, revealing a box from the jewelry store where they had found their wedding rings. Never in her life had anyone given her jewelry. Inside was a simple but elegant necklace: a small, glowing opal surrounded by tiny diamonds on a delicate chain. "Thank you."

"Do you like it? You could choose something else if you'd rather."

"No. It's perfect!"

"Are you sure?"

"Yes! I love it!" She smiled at him as they reached for one another's hands across the table.

"Caroline, I'm sorry we don't have the time to go somewhere special for our honeymoon. One week isn't enough to go to Europe or anywhere distant. And I can't afford a lot right now."

"I like what we planned!" Caroline objected. "Especially the first night in the cabin. It looks so nice."

"I hope it's as nice as it looks online," Peter commented.

"Well, I'm glad we're not spending a lot on the honeymoon. I don't think we can afford more and some of the places we chose look really nice."

"You're amazing," he said, rubbing her beautiful hands where they lay clasped in his. "I guess the less we spend now, the more we would have for a real trip later. Maybe next summer? In a year or two? A second honeymoon."

"I like that idea," Caroline approved. "That would give us time to save and to explore our options. I don't even know what I'd want to see in Europe."

"I guess I'm not sure either. Time to plan it would be good."

"That could be a lot of fun, actually!" agreed Caroline, imagining what it would be like to have a reason to research faraway places.

It was late by the time Peter walked her to her door.

"I don't think I'd better come in tonight," Peter said, giving her a lingering goodbye kiss. "I have an early class tomorrow but I don't want to leave."

"It's going to be nice to be married and get caught up on our sleep!" Caroline laughed.

"See you tomorrow," Peter said with one more goodbye kiss.

Caroline's days seemed to rush by with hardly enough hours to accomplish her coursework, senior project, and all of the wedding tasks. And then there were the themed evenings Peter kept coming up with to celebrate. On Monday it was Italian to the strains of romantic singing in words neither of them understood; on Tuesday Greek accompanied by a lively whirlwind of music; on Wednesday spicy Mexican food with mariachi, and on Thursday they grabbed burgers on the way to their next counseling session.

"Sorry about the lack of atmosphere," he apologized as they began to eat."

"Isn't that an old Peter, Paul, and Mary song?" Caroline asked, cocking her head to listen.

"It is!"

"Well, you can't get more American than hamburgers and old folk songs rendered nearly unrecognizable by synthesized blandness for your dining pleasure."

"You made me laugh!" Peter said, nearly choking on his French fries.

"You've made me laugh all week! Thanks for all the celebrating, by the way."

"My pleasure. I wonder what Pastor Clay has in mind for us tonight."

"I don't know," Caroline replied with a suddenly serious face.

"I don't think I would have had the courage to go through

with the first session if I'd known what was coming," Peter commented. "But I'm glad I did. I'm glad we did."

Caroline was surprised to hear Peter voice what she was thinking. She would have been far more nervous at the first session if she had known what they were about to experience. "It was unexpected but you're right: I think I learned a lot. Do you think there is more ahead?"

"More learning maybe, but I think we're done with the doubts," Peter said.

"Yes," Caroline stated emphatically.

Pastor Clay greeted them at the door with a broad smile and a welcoming handshake. "So glad I didn't scare you away," He said only half in jest.

"It *was* difficult. Difficult but wise of you," Peter assured him.

"I hope you've celebrated sufficiently to forgive me," he said with only a bit of a smile.

Caroline laughingly filled Clay and Julie in on the themed celebration Peter had provided each day.

"Well done, Peter! Tonight I want to talk about ways to keep our hearts tender toward one another. Jesus said that Moses allowed divorce because of the hardness of the human heart. It is not what God desires for us. For us to be happy with ourselves and one another we need to keep abiding in him. God has given you a wonderful gift by giving you one another, so I want to explore ways to nurture and grow that gift.

"I thought we'd start by reading Matthew 22:36-38. Peter, would you read those verses for us?" Pastor Clay asked.

Peter opened his Bible and read, '"Teacher, which is the greatest commandment in the Law?' Jesus replied, 'Love the Lord your God with all your heart and with all your soul and with all your mind. This is the first and greatest commandment.'"

Pastor Clay smiled. "I love this interchange between Jesus and the Pharisees who were trying to test Jesus in order to invalidate him. But there are many validations that Jesus was from God and that he was and is who he claimed to be. We can see some of those authentications in this passage.

One authentication is that Jesus used Old Testament Scripture accurately and truthfully. You see, Jesus is quoting Deuteronomy chapter 6 here. He quotes Deuteronomy 6:5 because it is a commandment from God. Perhaps because of who it was that asked the question, Jesus used 'mind' from the Greek translation of the Old Testament instead of 'strength'. Maybe the listeners in this particular group valued their minds above their strength. That's speculation on my part. Jesus knew their hearts at the time, and we don't. But this commandment is truth that was important to God from the very beginning. God made sure his people knew it was the bottom line required of them. Both Jesus and the Pharisees who were challenging him knew this commandment and its importance.

"Another authentication that Jesus is truthful and is from God is that Jesus always pointed people to the Father. Here in Matthew, when asked to name the greatest commandment, Jesus goes immediately to the command to love God above all else, with everything we are and have. Tonight, we'll be focusing on the first and greatest commandment and how that commandment to love God relates to marriage."

"Okay," Peter nodded.

"When Jesus says to love God with all our heart, soul, and mind he means with our whole being, but I find it helpful to define that by breaking it down into the parts. What does it really mean to love God with all our hearts in particular?"

"The heart has to do with affection and emotion," Caroline stated slowly. *This is going to take some thought!* "That means I'm to love God with everything that is involved with my emotions? With everything I'm attached to or value. More than anything that is precious to me?"

"That's what I would say, too," Peter agreed. "God is asking us to love him more than anything or anyone who might have a claim on our affections. To love him more than anything or anyone we are attached to."

"Sorry, but it reminds me again of Abraham being willing to offer up his beloved son, trusting that God would actually resurrect him," Caroline said. "It was something God had planned from the very beginning to do with his own Son, out of love for all of us."

"It's amazing isn't it?" Pastor Clay commented. "I'm amazed every time I think of that kind of love that God would have toward us. God never asks of us what he is unwilling to give on our behalf, or really, has already given."

"Ours seems like a poor imitation compared to what God has done," Peter commented.

"Yes, but God is generous. He counted Abraham's belief as righteousness. That's all that he requires of us," Pastor Clay reminded them. "And Abraham's faith became a great symbol of the sacrificial love God intended to show his fallen creation."

"I thought of Hannah, too," Caroline contributed. "I remember your sermon about her giving her son Samuel as a living sacrifice to God by giving him to God's service. I like the way you tied it to Romans chapter 12 where we are all expected to present ourselves as living sacrifices, living holy lives that are pleasing to God, as showing proper worship and reverence for God."

Peter nodded in agreement.

"Yes!" Pastor Clay affirmed. "The way we live our lives hopefully shows that we love him with all our heart. How about our souls?"

My soul. Caroline was silent. Wasn't that the eternal part of her? The part that was authentically her? The part that lived forever. *How can I love God with all my soul?* "Maybe it has to do with preparing our souls to spend eternity in God's presence?"

"That's a good connection!" Peter exclaimed. "It is a tough question that makes me think. So, to continue with the connection that Caroline has made, maybe it has to do with sanctifying ourselves? Setting ourselves apart to God?"

"I like the connections you're both making." Pastor Clay encouraged. "Determining to live a holy life doesn't mean trying to live a perfect life. It means dedicating our life to service to God."

"In this life and in the life to come?" Caroline questioned.

"I suppose so," Peter realized. "Serving God in this life prepares us for his presence, and is good practice for serving him in the next life. It makes heaven a little more real to think of doing things in heaven to help God's kingdom come to earth. An extension of our service here in this life. Not just worshipping and playing harps. I don't know…"

Pastor Clay commented, "We don't really know, of course. Practicing worship *now* before coming into his literal presence is probably good preparation, as well as practicing service to him. How about loving God with all our minds?"

"There must be a connection to our souls, because when I think of loving God with my mind, I think of sanctifying my thoughts. Setting aside thoughts that don't honor God. And practicing being in his presence," Peter replied.

"How interesting to think of loving God in these ways as preparation to being in his actual presence!" Caroline exclaimed.

"I like the way you two think," Pastor Clay said with a smile. "We're going to add the fourth component since Jesus includes it in the book of Mark. How do we love God with all our strength?"

"That seems a little easier," Caroline commented. "I think it means that I should expend even my physical strength on God's work, on his priorities."

"Yes," Peter continued, "and other kinds of effort as well, I suppose. Our hardest efforts physically, mentally, in every way, should be directed toward obeying God and serving him."

"It's a little overwhelming," Caroline admitted.

"Yes, it is," Peter agreed. "It makes me question if I'm really loving God."

"That's good, but I don't want either of you to grow discouraged. This week, I'd like you to memorize Matthew 22:37-40 if you haven't already. In addition, I'd like you to answer these questions on your own, without consulting one another. Does my life show my love for God? How could my life best show my love for God? Please write down how you think that should look in your own life. Make it practical but not impossible to live up to. We'll discuss your answers together next week and you can share your vision for a godly life, then, with each other. If you can back your answers up with other Scripture, that would be great. Oh, and when you're answering this week's questions, you're not allowed to include anything about how loving God helps us love one another. We'll save that for next week. So, the focus is all on God. Remember not to make it about one another. Don't write what you think your future spouse wants or expects. This is between you and God."

"So, is there anything we can do for the two of you?" Julie asked. "How are the wedding plans coming along?"

"Pretty well," Caroline replied with a smile in Peter's direction. I think we've almost got it covered. We were able to make a decision about the wedding cake, thanks to you!"

"I'm afraid I'm asking a lot of Caroline," Peter said. "I didn't give her much time to plan this event."

"How are you feeling about that? Are you feeling rushed?" Pastor Clay asked Caroline.

"It's a good kind of rush," Caroline smiled. "I'm kind of glad I don't have more time to focus on more minor things."

"Are you happy with the arrangements?" Julie asked. "Or do you feel like you're cutting corners and missing out on some things you would like to have as part of your memories?"

"I think I'm pretty happy with the way things are shaping up. My wedding dress is an answer to prayer and I really like the flowers we've chosen. I'm glad we're doing the traditional rehearsal and rehearsal dinner, thanks to Peter's parents. I love the venue they found."

"That's good," Julie said. "Our biggest piece of wedding

advice is that it's best to accept that something is bound to go askew on *The Day*! So, when it does, just let it go rather than getting upset about it and letting it spoil everything. In fact, the nicest thing you can do for yourselves is to ask another couple to be host and hostess at the wedding to take all that off your hands. It's best if you aren't hurrying around making sure everything is in place before the wedding. That way you can enjoy and appreciate your wedding day."

"That sounds like a good idea," Caroline said, astounded at the new idea. "What do you think, Peter?"

"Sounds good to me."

"We'll have to think about who could do that."

"Someone you trust who is not involved with too many other duties in the service," Julie advised.

"And how about the actual service? Do you have any specific requests about what you'd like me to include?" asked Pastor Clay.

"We have talked about it. We do want you to emphasize that we are entering into a covenant before God." Caroline looked at Peter for corroboration.

"Yes, a real marriage vow. Not just telling one another how much in love we are. I like what you said about our love being a gift from God." Peter said. "Should we include that?" he asked, turning to Caroline.

"Yes. I like that. Can you do that, Pastor Clay?"

"Absolutely."

"I really want it to be a witness to any students who come who don't know Christ." Caroline glanced up at Pastor Clay. "Will you make sure to include the plan of salvation?"

"I'm more than happy to oblige. I like to include it as part of the explanation of what Christian marriage represents."

"Thank you!" Caroline was hopeful it would find resonance with someone in the audience who didn't really understand what it meant to be a Christian.

"I'll email the whole ceremony to each of you so you can tweak it if you want, including a rough draft of my comments for you to look at."

"Thank you, Pastor Clay," Peter said, shaking his hand. "Since Caroline has made my grandparents' church her home, I look forward to making it mine. Thank you for the counseling and for doing the ceremony."

"My pleasure."

"I think I'm going to enjoy this man's ministry in my life," Peter commented once they were in the car. "I think I could go to him with any spiritual question and get godly counsel."

"I like the way he asks questions and lets us wrestle with the answers ourselves."

"Yes."

"What you said made me think about this life being practice for living with God forever. I think practicing humility now, worshipping God, serving him—aren't those things that will prepare us for eternity with him?"

"I think so," Peter replied. "Loving God with all our being makes me think of Daniel. He continued to pray to God when it was forbidden by law. God saved him from death in the lions' den. And then his three friends Shadrach, Meshach, and Abednego wouldn't worship the king even though they knew it meant death. They knew God was the only one we should worship."

"I like what the three men said when they were threatened with death," Caroline commented.

"That God could deliver them from the fiery furnace, but even if he didn't, they would not bow down and worship the king?"

"Yes! And God did deliver them!" Caroline exclaimed.

"Yes," said Peter. "He delivered them in such a way that no one could deny it was God's power. Not even a whiff of smoke or scorching on them when they came out!"

"I love that Jesus came into the furnace with them to free them and they were all walking around unharmed in the fire." Caroline was grinning.

"It is wonderful," agreed Peter.

"And I love that Nebuchadnezzar couldn't do anything but praise God and decree that anyone speaking against their God would lose his life," Caroline added with a glowing face.

Peter looked admiringly at Caroline and silently thanked

the Lord for her and for the way God was working in their lives. He looked forward to their joint efforts at trying to serve God with everything they had, and with everything they were, and with all that they might become.

⚘ CHAPTER FIVE ⚘

Jo had scheduled a bridal shower for Caroline on Friday evening, just a personal one with her best friends. Caroline dreaded the jokes, the games, and the gifts, but she asked God to help her through what she was sure would be an embarrassing evening. She could only hope that her Christian friends would be discreet. Jo's grandparents, John and Martha, had offered to make themselves scarce so they could have the shower at their house next door. Caroline headed over after a quick meal of steak and beans, provided by Peter in a cowboy hat! While Caroline cleaned up the kitchen, Peter took off his hat and went into the library to measure and decide what pieces would work best in Caroline's new office. She had chosen some different online furniture that was very compatible with the beautiful built-ins of the library, but it had taken Peter a lot of effort to convinced her that even these items weren't too expensive. Peter's reasoning that they were half the cost of having something custom made had finally convinced her. Fortunately the two of them had been able to check out the office furniture and cabinets on display at the local store. He really did think what they intended to order would be just as high quality as having someone come in to build them. The ones they had chosen were expensive but worth it in the long run.

They measured and discussed which pieces would be most useful and arrangements that would look the most like built-ins. They were both relieved to be able to come to decisions about what they felt would work the best before parting—Peter to finalize the list of pieces and double check the measurements while Caroline jogged next door.

Caroline was the first one to arrive at the shower but Jo had already decorated the living room with the wedding colors.

"Have a good time!" said Grandma Martha as she and Grandpa John went out the door.

"Thank you! I'm sorry to kick you out of your own house!" Caroline exclaimed.

"I'm not!" grinned Grandma Martha. "He hasn't taken me out to dinner in a long time."

"Good excuse for a date," agreed Grandpa John with a smile and a wink.

"They are so cute!" Caroline commented to Jo when they were gone.

"They are, aren't they? Just like you and Peter will be," she teased.

"By the way," Caroline said, "how are you managing to get your coursework done? You really don't have to do so much for us."

"I'm glad the seminary's not far from home. That helps. And I'm actually not taking a full load this semester. Matt is, but I'm kind of glad I'm not."

"How is Matt?" Caroline was sure any mention of Matt would always take her back to her very uncomfortable time at the city mission when she was supposedly helping Jo and her Christian friends serve the needy and bring the gospel to them. Matt's sermon that day had made the gospel clear to *her*!

"He's fine. We try to do something together other than studying, at least once in a while."

"Real dates? Dress up and go to dinner dates?" Caroline couldn't help but ask since Jo had been so intentional on Caroline's behalf for Peter's dress-up date on her birthday.

"No! We're trying to do inexpensive casual things like hiking and cycling. It's good for us to take a break from studying and neither of us wants to rush things at this point. Seminary pretty much takes everything we've got."

"That and planning all of these wedding-related events!"

"But it's such fun! I wouldn't miss it!"

The evening turned out to be a lot more fun than Caroline expected. She was actually thankful for the fineness of the negligees that she never would have purchased for herself.

She had already secretly decided which one to wear on the wedding night. When Jo ended the evening by asking the girls to gather around Caroline to pray for her and Peter and their marriage, Caroline was blessed to her core and couldn't keep the grateful tears from her eyes. This was not your typical bridal shower!

The days rushed by and, in spite of the meaningful counsel, Caroline had to admit to herself that she would be relieved to be finished with the counseling sessions. On Thursday evening, they discussed the answers to the questions about putting God first as a means of demonstrating their love for him.

Caroline was hesitant about sharing her answers, especially when she was asked to go first. When she glanced at her written answers they seemed inadequate to explain what she had really been thinking so she tried to explain.

"I was thinking of I John 4:19. We love God because he first loved us. This week when I practiced telling the Lord that I love him, I ended up just basking in his presence, in *his* love, because I realized that my love was a response to all the love he has shown to me."

"Go on," encouraged Pastor Clay.

"I guess it seems to me that's where I have to start each day. Even if I'm not feeling love for God, stopping and taking the time to express my love for him adjusts my priorities in life and helps me to carry his love for me into my day. I know we're not talking about loving others yet, but accepting God's love is the only way I can even begin to hope to show his love to others."

"That's okay! You're so right! Let's hold that thought." He turned to Peter and asked what he had written about.

"I thought of Colossians 3:23 that says whatever we are doing, we should do it wholeheartedly as though our work was for the Lord. I think that's because whatever a Christian is doing, it really *is* for the Lord." He went on to talk about how he had dedicated his mind to God and that all of his studying was done to bring glory to God. He hoped to use his degrees and opportunities to bring the gospel to business people. Then he went on to say that he was also very deliberate about keeping his thoughts holy and pleasing to God.

"And with good reason," commented Pastor Clay. "Our actions rise out of our heart and mind. What we *do* is a result of what we think and believe and let our minds dwell on."

After some discussion about how important our thoughts were to our actions, Pastor Clay asked his next question. "Why do you think Jesus said this kind of love for God is the first and greatest commandment? Caroline, your turn. What you said earlier was related to this."

"Well, I remember when I realized that God actually created me and cared about me and loved me, it totally changed my outlook. I had to decide whether to respond to that. When I recognized that God had been active in my life and wanted to show his love to me, I was so amazed! I guess that's why I was able to ask Jesus to forgive me and come in and live in me. Now, every day I need his help to love God the way I should and to put him first. Somehow, when I spend time with him he is with me through the day. When I don't spend time with him before starting my day, things don't work so well."

"So, what do you think, Peter? Why is that?"

"If we aren't focused on loving God and putting him first, then we end up living for ourselves and not for him and his purposes. We aren't available to him and God's kingdom isn't advanced. At least that's what happens to me. If I put him first, then my thoughts and goals and actions are more likely to align with his instead of disappointing him and working against him."

"So there's no neutral ground? If we're not for him, we're against him?" asked Pastor Clay.

"I would say that's true," Peter replied.

"It reminds me of King Josiah in the Old Testament," commented Pastor Clay. "He was a later King of Judah. By the time he became king, no one even remembered the Book of the Law and what God required of his people. When he discovered how far they had gone away from God's instructions, he had an enormous job to do. Previous kings, as far back as Solomon, had constructed idols and worship places for foreign gods. They were not wholehearted in their worship of God. As a result, the people of God got farther and farther away from God. When Josiah read the book that had been rediscovered in the temple and learned what God had told his people, he instigated repentance and set about destroying those idols and places to worship other gods. I think he's a good example of loving God with all your strength. It took considerable strength of purpose to actually demolish all of those things that were so detestable to God and provide the leadership to turn the nation back to God." Pastor Clay paused.

"So, I guess it's pretty important not to allow our lives to become filled with things that don't honor God," Caroline observed.

"Yes. God requires us to forsake all other gods to follow him. So, what does all of this have to do with marriage?" asked Pastor Clay.

"I'm thinking of the marriage vows about forsaking all others," Peter commented.

"Good point. That's pretty basic to a successful marriage," Pastor Clay agreed. "If you are each committed to giving up all others who are attractive to you, both now and as long as you both shall live, in sickness and in health, for richer, for poorer, then your marriage will endure. Let's move on to other ways this relates to marriage."

There was a pause while Peter and Caroline gathered their thoughts.

"If we are both single minded about serving God, about putting him first, we will have a lot less friction and disagreement in our marriage," Caroline commented.

"True. But differences will still arise. Sometimes Christians can become very opinionated and rigid and believe they are right because they believe they are putting God first. They can become destructive to those closest to them and to the body of Christ if they are not governed by love. The same could happen in a marriage. So is it about being right?"

"No," Peter said. "If love is governing our relationship, then we are more focused on blessing and helping one another than proving we're right."

Caroline said thoughtfully, "It reminds me of your comment last week about avoiding hardness of heart. When people harden their hearts toward God, it can't be good for their life or the people around them."

"That's probably a good segue to our topic for next time. Next week, let's see what you think about loving others as yourself and how that relates to marriage,"

Before leaving, they discussed the marriage ceremony and Pastor Clay's intended comments. Caroline felt relieved when it was finalized. It was going to be perfect! She hoped.

Julie, as though reading her thoughts, asked, "Did you think of anyone to act as host and hostess to help with the unexpected?"

"Oh, Peter!" Caroline exclaimed, "I was wondering what

you'd think of asking Jenn and Patrick."

"Patrick, the associate pastor who oversees the ministry to young families?"

"Yes."

"I don't know them. I mean we've met but I don't know much about them."

"You're right. I'm having a hard time coming up with someone."

"But they might be a good choice! It might be a good way to get to know them a little better. After all, we'll soon be in that category! " Peter commented.

"What do you think?" Caroline asked Julie.

"I think that's a great choice. It might be best if they have a babysitter so they can be focused on the wedding. Their little guy is too young to appreciate a wedding."

"Oh, you're right. It seems like a lot to ask. They're so busy. Is there someone else?" Caroline wondered with a frown.

"What if we paid for their babysitter?" Peter suggested.

"Great idea!" Julie exclaimed. "They really would be a good choice. I think they would do a great job and I'm sure they would enjoy the chance to be of help. Would you like me to ask them?"

"That would be wonderful!" Caroline replied.

"I'm happy to do that," Julie said. "I can fill them in on what they should watch for to divert pressure from you and your bridal party and relatives. It's a good way for them to get to know *you*."

"Wow! That sounds really great! Thank you!" Peter said. "You can fill us in on what they'll be covering so we don't have to."

"That's the idea. Everyone involved in the wedding should be able to enjoy the day," Julie said with a smile.

On the way home, Peter voiced what was in Caroline's mind. "The wedding is two weeks from Saturday!"

Caroline put her hand to her forehead, thinking of all she needed to do in the next two weeks. "Speaking of Saturday, I think I'm going to have to finish up some coursework this Saturday. With the shower tomorrow night at your parents' I don't see how I can be ready for next week without some hours on Saturday."

"I have some major projects to grade this weekend, too."

"Maybe we could see how things are looking by midafternoon Saturday. We could at least have dinner together Saturday night."

"Okay, but we need to order the cabinets for your office and I want your final okay. You're bringing your lunch to my office tomorrow, right?" Peter asked.

"Umm… sure."

Caroline was tired by the time Peter said goodbye. She needed to sleep. She was basically ready for tomorrow and anything else would just have to wait.

After their hurried lunch in Peter's university office the next day, he stopped on his way out to say, "I'll pick you up at six tonight for the shower. We can stop for a bite on the way," They had looked again at the cabinet pieces Peter had fitted into the space available, based on his measurements and the information online. Caroline wished briefly that she'd taken just a moment that morning to peek into the library so she had a fresh picture of it in her mind. There was no doubt that what they were planning would definitely be an improvement in function and convenience for her. Would it look like it really fit? Would her extended presence in the library have the result of more opportunity to use the reading chairs and play the piano, or would it spoil the special feeling she'd always had for the room?

Later that afternoon when she let herself into the house and closed the front door behind her, she leaned back against it to catch her breath. She had looked forward to this moment of homecoming all day. Her love for the house and for the special people who had prayed for her and left it to her made it her own sanctuary. When she was there, in the quiet peace and solitude of her home, she felt the presence of the Lord. This was where she retreated to recharge. Would it continue to be a sanctuary to her when Peter was sharing the space? Maybe it had become *too much* of a sanctuary. She remembered how lonely the house had felt when she had given up on Peter ever sharing it with her. She was so much happier now. Tired but happy.

When she and Peter arrived at his parents' home that evening, they found it full of people from Peter's church and from Caroline's. Not everyone invited to the wedding had been invited to the shower, but many of Peter's parents' friends and many of Grandma and Grandpa Lockwood's oldest friends were there with the result that Peter knew most but not all of them and Caroline knew some of them. She knew many of the Lockwood's friends from her church and she had met some of those present who attended Peter's church as well. It was an older crowd, and larger, than Jo had assembled for Caroline's personal shower. This was meant to be a general shower that included Peter. She was sure she needn't worry about the gifts or the kidding with this group.

It was a lovely evening full of generosity and well wishes. Since they would live in the home Caroline's grandparents had left her, there was little they would need in terms of setting up housekeeping. They had resisted registering for gifts until Peter's parents pointed out that there would be gifts, regardless, and they might as well receive things that they would find useful and beautiful. Caroline realized as she inventoried what was in the house that new sheets and towels would be helpful. Peter had come up with things that would be helpful in the garage and yard.

Many of the men had watched Peter grow up and enjoyed kidding him about the chain saw and other yard maintenance items he had requested. Several of them had gotten together to purchase the items, and the jokes about the jungle surrounding their future home began to fly. There were also a few items that Caroline had to admit were not what she would have chosen, items that would not fit with the house or her color palette, and even one rather garish gift; but that was to be expected as everyone had different tastes and preferences. Caroline took great joy in opening a few very special gifts from those who had traveled extensively. There were a couple of elegant vases that she looked forward to adding to her flower-arranging room. Most of all, she was grateful and overwhelmed by the generosity and acceptance of these family friends. She felt very blessed.

Saturday was filled with work and a relaxing dinner together followed by more work, separately, in order for Peter and Caroline to be able to enjoy time together on Sunday. The week was filled with more work as both students and professors were attempting to prepare for spring break. When Thursday rolled around, they grabbed another quick burger on the way to the last counseling session.

"Thank you for talking to Jenn and Patrick," Caroline said to Julie as they entered.

"Oh, did they contact you?"

"Yes. Jenn called me and Patrick called Peter. We're all set."

"Great! Good choice. I think they'll do a great job as wedding host and hostess!"

They talked that evening about what it meant to love others as one's self. It meant, first of all, not to do harm to others since we do not enjoy it when someone else does harm to us. It meant seeing the potential in other people, even difficult people, and trying to see them through God's eyes. It meant putting other people's needs front and center instead of focusing only on our own needs. It meant asking God, in some cases, for his love to shine through to difficult people and for his help to develop love for them. It meant praying for others and finding practical ways to help them.

"So, it's pretty easy to see the connection to marriage here," Pastor Clay said. "I encourage you to practice this with one another every day at home. At times, it can actually be more difficult to practice this kind of humility with your spouse and your family than with others. It's challenging because of the quantity of time you spend with one another, because of how well you know and experience each other's weaknesses, and because of the intensity of marriage. So it takes purposeful commitment to try to live consistently with the person you are closest to, even when you love that person.

"To finish tonight and to conclude our counseling sessions, I'd like to take us to Ephesians chapter 5. You will probably hear many sermons in your lifetime about this passage. It gives some practical ways to walk 'in the way of love' by following God's example. Let's read the entire chapter to ourselves. I'll give you a few minutes and ask you to concentrate on the overall context as you read."

When they had finished reading, Pastor Clay continued.

"The last verse in the previous chapter is important here. 'Be kind and compassionate to one another, forgiving each other, just as in Christ God forgave you.' It provides an introduction to what follows, a reminder of how much God has forgiven us. Why do you think that could be key to loving others and especially to a strong marriage?"

"It humbles me to think of how much God has forgiven in me," Caroline responded. "He does that for everyone who calls on him. He forgives generously."

"Yes," Julie agreed. "And I'm afraid the longer we live, even after committing our lives to Jesus, the more we realize how much we need, and continue to need, God's forgiveness."

"The apostle Paul reminds his readers that Jesus cares a great deal about his body, the church, the people who represent him here and now on earth. He wants us to walk in God's love, to live up to our calling, to reflect the character of Christ. Unfortunately, none of us is perfect and at different points in your marriage you will be blessed if you simply forgive. It is easier to forgive what may seem like enormous affronts if we keep our own shortcomings in mind along with the continued forgiveness our heavenly Father offers to us. Because men and women see things differently, it is easy to take offence rather than to back off and pray about

93

differences; but if we can do that, God can work things out for us in a peaceful way that we couldn't do on our own."

"I hope I don't turn out to be an old bachelor stuck in my ways!" Peter exclaimed. He turned to Caroline. "Forgive me ahead of time and have patience with me!"

"I might ask you to do the same for me," Caroline laughed.

"So, this passage that follows about submission can be sticky," Pastor Clay commented, "but the two of you have just expressed exactly the way to find your way through it. What does verse 21 say?"

"Submit to one another out of reverence for Christ," Peter read.

"So who submits to whom?" asked Pastor Clay.

"We submit to one another," Peter said with a thoughtful frown.

"That's not easy," Pastor Clay observed. "Why do we bother? According to this verse, why try to do that?"

"Out of reverence for Christ," Caroline said.

Pastor Clay continued. "This passage is not about women submitting to men. It's about the body of Christ living in mutual submission. And that's especially applicable in marriage as it is in the other relationships Paul mentions as he continues in chapter 6."

"Mutual submission," mused Peter. "I'm assuming it takes a lifetime of marriage to sort that out."

Pastor Clay laughed. "I think you're right. Marriage is the great proving ground for what we say we believe, but if we can master ourselves (Not one another. Ourselves!) in that intimate, intense setting, we have a good chance of living out Christ's principles in our broader life."

They ended their premarital counseling in prayer and eager conversation about wedding details.

Friday. One more week to go!

Caroline tried her newly-tailored wedding gown on and loved the results. The house was as ready as it could be, and she loved the new paint in the bedroom. Peter would bring clothes to the closet next week, but if they didn't get it all moved in it didn't really matter. They could finish later, but they were trying to get set up so that they could jump back into school after the honeymoon. She was really glad that Jenn and Patrick would be on the job to see that the flowers and the cake arrived Saturday morning so she wouldn't have to worry about anything after putting on her wedding dress. Still, she would check on everything before dressing for the wedding. *Oops! One more call to the florist to cover Jenn and Patrick!*

༶༶༶

The Friday evening rehearsal was going slowly but smoothly through the traditional order of service until Pastor Clay looked up to see Caroline coming up the aisle on the arm of Grandpa John Lockwood, with Dr. Calton and Grandpa Sam Larson marching jubilantly, but silently, behind them. They were obviously hardly able to contain their mirth.

"Who gives this woman to this man?" the pastor asked with a quirked eyebrow.

"*We* do!" they all shouted in chorus.

When the laughter had died down, Pastor Clay said dryly, "Perhaps it would be better if just one of you answered the question."

"We know. We just had to do it once! Go ahead, John," Dr. Calton said while everyone laughed again.

"As honored representatives of Caroline's parents and grandparents, Mrs. Lockwood and I do," Grandpa John said, exactly as planned.

The rest of the rehearsal was all the more joyous and, since it would be a very traditional service, seemed easy to get through. Peter and Caroline had gone through the ceremony with the pastor to update the language in ways that made sense to them and would clarify the meaning of the ceremony. They knew what he would say in his brief explanation of what Christian marriage was intended to represent. They had decided on private written messages to be exchanged with one another before the ceremony, so that the service would proceed in an unbroken progression. They preferred to keep their innermost feelings for one another to themselves as a private, holy time that they could talk about as husband and wife. They wanted the public ceremony to point to Christ.

Grandpa John and Grandmother Martha had insisted on helping Peter's parents with the rehearsal dinner at a quiet but elegant restaurant that a friend of theirs had recommended. Large, round tables set with china and flowers filled the room. Caroline could not have been happier. While the wedding party began to arrive, she and Peter enjoyed taking in the view from the large windows. Caroline could see their reflection, Peter's arm caressingly enclosing her. She stored the memory. Forever.

Peter, however, was not content with a reflection, and turning toward Caroline, much to everyone's satisfaction, he leaned in for a romantic kiss, a long one. Caroline was embarrassed, as he knew she would be, but this amazing woman was about to become his wife! He could hardly be more in love.

Peter's father took the opportunity after all of the laughter and teasing that followed, to invite them all to find their name places and be seated.

"I believe the staff would like to begin serving dinner, so let's begin with a word of thanks to the Lord for this wonderful occasion." He waited for the guests to settle. "Lord Jesus, we welcome you here with us. We express our gratitude for the great sacrifice you made on our behalf. We bless you for your willingness to rescue us from our sin and its consequences. We bless you for choosing to walk with us, to bear our burdens, to shepherd us, to show us how to live by loving you and loving others instead of living in our own selfishness. And now, Lord you have given a great, unselfish love to Peter and Caroline, and we are grateful. We are grateful for the way you have worked in their lives, and we are grateful, knowing that they desire you to be the center of their marriage and their life together. We ask you to bless that desire, to walk with them through every day and every night. We ask that their marriage and life together would greatly honor you and point many to a new way of life. May their marriage be blessed with all the blessings of heaven above and the beautiful earth below where we have the honor of living ever before your face and in your presence. We give you all the glory and praise and honor, now and forevermore."

Caroline wiped tears from her eyes, hardly able to bear the blessing Peter's father had bestowed upon them. Somehow, now, this meal with all of their closest and dearest ones present became something more than a party. What a blessing that Peter's father and mother had raised him to know and walk with the Lord! She was confident that Peter would continue to invite Jesus' presence into their home.

The meal was superb. Caroline looked forward to seeing the photographs being taken by the wedding photographer.

Jo, of course, plus all of Caroline's university friends, and Peter's friends and family blended into one festive celebration. There were no toasts at this party, and no need for them because the guests would not expect alcohol to be present. There were, however, plenty of good wishes and prayers for the soon-to-be-newlyweds.

It was late and most of the guests were long gone when Peter noticed that Caroline was looking tired. "Shall I take you home? How about we ask Jo to ride with us?"

"That would be nice."

It was something Jo had committed to do whenever Peter knew it might be a good idea to have a chaperone. Caroline was looking quite beautiful in his eyes at the moment and the wedding was tomorrow!

"I have something for you," Caroline said as he prepared to say goodbye at her door. She handed him a small, wrapped box.

"Cufflinks! Fancy gold ones. These must have been expensive! Thank you! And monogramed! As a lowly professor, I don't know if I need such grandeur."

"I know some were provided with the tux shirt you rented for the wedding, but they aren't very nice. Now you have your own. Maybe you'll need them again sometime."

"Whether I ever wear them again or not, thank you. I happen to have something for you as well, you know." Peter said, handing her a small, nicely-wrapped gift.

Caroline was puzzled. *What? Another jewelry box? But we have our rings. I can't imagine.* She opened the white hinged jewelry case and exclaimed. "Peter! It's beautiful!" A single stunning teardrop pearl was topped by a bright sparkle of diamond where it joined the chain. "Now I don't know which necklace to wear tomorrow! Thank you!"

"Will it work with the wedding dress?"

"It would work with any dress! Yes, it will be just the thing! But you've already given me a necklace. I've never had such beautiful jewelry!"

"I thought you should have options for tomorrow."

Caroline couldn't help but wonder if someone had given him a tip about the dress, but she didn't want to say anything to give away the style of her wedding dress.

"You seem to like pearls," Peter stated hopefully.

"How do you know?"

"All of those fake pearls you chose to include with the flowers."

"I see!" she laughed. "Don't you like them?" she queried.

"Sure. I just thought you should have some of the real thing."

She tried not to be hurt. Did he think the fake ones hanging from the flowers were lacking in taste?

"We don't have to have the pearls with the flowers."

"No. They're fine!" Peter protested.

She preferred to conclude that either Peter was very kind

in perceiving that she liked pearls, or that someone like Jo had given him a tip about the dress. If she had the chance to ask Jo sometime, she wasn't sure whether she would or not. Maybe she could ask Peter sometime. At any rate, she chose to believe that the wedding would be truly beautiful and set it aside, reminding herself that it was not the time to worry about what other people would think! She was still convinced that it would be more beautiful than any wedding she could have imagined for herself.

CHAPTER SIX

The morning of the wedding, Caroline's time was spent trying to get her hair and veil to look the way she imagined it should. She had thought it would be an easy thing to accomplish on her own. So, after giving herself a free manicure and pedicure, she tried on the veil. The tailor had sewn the new veil to her grandmother's intricately beaded headpiece and Caroline had liked the results. At least, at the time it had seemed right. Now that the day had arrived, she just couldn't get the headpiece to sit right or the veil to flow correctly in what should be a becoming way. It took several attempts for her to get her hair arranged in near approximation to what she had imagined, and it still wasn't exactly right, but it was time to drive to the church where they would all dress in their appropriate wedding attire. After that, she would be stuck with whatever the veil chose to do. She calmly reminded herself of Julie's wise counsel that something was bound to not quite measure up and she was able to remain calm. She prayed that all would be well with the bridesmaids, the guys' tuxes, the flowers, refreshments, and the multitude of other things that could go wrong. There were so many stories circulating about things like the groom's pants splitting just before the ceremony or the cake being stale that she could only pray that all would be well. She didn't want their wedding to become one of those stories. The wedding hostess was well equipped with a complete sewing kit and if the cake was stale, there was nothing to be done now. Julie was right: all that really mattered at this point was that they enjoy this monumental day in their lives.

It was incredibly fun to be with all the bridesmaids as they prepared to look their best. They all looked lovely, of course, and Caroline could only thank them and silently thank God for the amazing ways he had brought them together and used their gifts as individuals and as believers to enhance her life. She was grateful for each one.

Sandwiches and lemonade were provided for all of the wedding party and helpers in their respective areas and eaten with relish and great care. Caroline didn't want to eat once she had her dress on, but the girls helped her cover it, encouraging her not to become dehydrated, leading to a faint; or to become so hungry that her stomach growled during the ceremony! They laughed at the outrageous possibilities that arose with those thoughts and very soon they had finished, touched up their lipstick, smoothed their hair, and were ready for the photographs when it was their turn in front of the cameras. The wedding photographer had already done Peter and his family and the groomsmen and then they had withdrawn to another area of the church. When all of the photos except for the combined bride and groom and wedding party were finished, it seemed to take a long time for the wedding guests to arrive. But the time came when Caroline and the bridesmaids filed out into the reception room at the back of the church. Grandpa John seemed so excited to see her that Caroline hoped he could make it through the ceremony without a faux pas.

"We couldn't be happier for Peter," he whispered as they stood out of sight, waiting for their turn.

"Thank you, Grandpa John, for everything," Caroline whispered back, taking his arm.

And then, there she was, standing in the doorway at the end of the aisle, waiting for the organist to begin the wedding march. She couldn't look at Peter's grinning face and, instead, chose to concentrate on walking carefully and demurely beside Grandpa John what seemed like a great distance before taking her place in front of the "altar" which was merely a table, but a table with great meaning. It was here that Pastor Clay regularly blessed his congregation by serving communion as it represented Christ's sacrifice of his body and blood on their behalf. She tried to focus on what Pastor Clay was saying. Though she was as happy as she could imagine any bride being on her wedding day, she was

105

secretly terrified of fainting or stumbling or making a wrong move in front of all of these people! She was glad the ceremony was being recorded so that she could enjoy it later.

She concentrated on breathing normally and staying relaxed, and tried to listen as Pastor Clay worked his way toward the central message that marriage was intended to represent the great love Jesus has for his followers. As such, it placed a great responsibility on those who joined their lives together in a covenant that mirrored God's covenant of never-ending love for the followers of Jesus.

"God promises such love through Jesus, his beloved son. The promise is made out of the love the Father has for that only, precious Son who was willing to give up everything, willing to endure every imaginable agony in order to win forgiveness and peace with God for his own rebellious creation. That is what Christian marriage is intended to show to the world. Unconditional love."

Caroline fought back tears, so deeply thankful for God's unconditional love and for Peter's unconditional love. She prayed that anyone present who had not accepted God's gift of love through his Son would hear and understand and be led by God's Spirit to believe and receive it.

Pastor Clay prayed, "Heavenly Father, your Word tells us that a cord of three strands is not easily broken. Peter and Caroline make a strong cord together, but we ask you to be that third strand, strengthening and sustaining them, together."

They each repeated the traditional wedding vows and before she knew it, Caroline had received Peter's ardent kiss and they were introduced as Mr. and Mrs. Peter Berkhardt. The photographer captured their brilliant smiles just before exuberant organ music filled the room, signaling the completion of the ceremony and their recessional back down the aisle, this time as a married couple.

They stood at the back greeting everyone as the guests came out, and then retreated to the sanctuary with the bridal party for the final important pictures before proceeding to the cake cutting. Caroline was relieved when the cake proved as delicious as it had at the cake tasting. Thankfully, the guests would not have to endure dry cake!

The reception was filled with well wishes, and Peter and Caroline discreetly completed their mission of thanking each participant as they moved from group to group. Eventually, they made their way to the front door where Peter's car, appropriately decorated, awaited them. They ran the gauntlet of bird seed, tossed with special vigor by all of the children and more gently by many of the adults, and the bridal party withdrew to change their bridal finery for more practical clothing before assembling with Peter's family at his parents' house where they all relaxed and watched Peter and Caroline open wedding gifts. Later, Jo and their parents would take the gifts to Caroline's house, now Peter's home also!

Evening approached before the newlyweds were able to

drive away in Caroline's MG where their packed suitcases awaited them. A week all to themselves!

※

By the end of that week, Caroline was happier than she had ever been and felt thoroughly married indeed. On Friday morning they headed for home, both eager to begin their new life together. For two days they slept in, settled in, and enjoyed their home. Sunday brought a full schedule of church and friends and joyous connecting with family. And Monday morning was the beginning of their busy future as husband and wife. They were committed to doing their best in their professional standings but both also worked hard to do their best for one another.

Weekends were a gift from God and never long enough, but they clung to the assurance that the semester would end soon and managed to finish out the school year in good shape. Caroline was relieved to graduate with her bachelor's degree and enjoyed celebrating the event with Peter, family, and friends. She had chosen to extend her master's so that she wouldn't have to take classes during the summer term. She was very ready to enjoy the summer!

"How about we open that safe today?" asked Peter one Saturday morning.

"Have you figured it out?"

"I think so."

"Wow! However did you do it?"

"Let's not count our chickens before they're hatched. I haven't actually opened it yet."

"But what have you found out?"

"I was able to research the types of safes the company installed and discovered that one of their choices was a safe hidden by a framed work of art. You unlock the picture with a long, thin key like this," he said, taking it from his pocket.

"Where did you find it? It doesn't even look like a key," Caroline said as she examined the odd-looking, slender piece of metal.

"That's the beauty of this kind of safe. I found it on your grandfather's key chain. Do you remember?"

"Yes. I gave you all of his keys so you could figure out what they belonged to. I think I thought this was some kind of a tool."

"Well, let's go see if it's the tool to move that picture!"

Caroline waited breathlessly while Peter felt carefully behind the right corner of the frame and then inserted the long, skinny key. She heard a click and the framed print swung out, revealing a small safe.

"What about the combination? Have you found it?"

"I believe I have. On a tiny, tiny piece of paper that was in your grandfather's side table."

"You mean with all of that stuff I put in a box? It's a good thing I didn't throw it away!"

109

"Yes, it is! I believe it is also written on the inside back cover of your grandmother's last journal."

"Is it really? There were a lot of blank pages at the end."

"True. And you had no reason to look. I, on the other hand, was curious and was reading with a more detached outlook."

"True," said Caroline with a frown.

"Understandable. I believe you should be the one to open this."

Caroline carefully turned the dial as Peter read the numbers from a small slip of paper.

"It worked!" Caroline exclaimed.

Inside were several envelopes containing birth certificates and death certificates for members of Caroline's family. There were also a few pieces of very old jewelry with sentimental meaning for her grandmother, according to the brief notes that accompanied them.

Caroline opened a jewelry box and exclaimed over a necklace of small, graduated pearls.

She unfolded a note and read,

> *For Caroline:*
> *These are the pearls I wore at our wedding.*
> *They were a gift from your grandfather. I'm*
> *sorry I've had to sell so much of my jewelry.*
> *May God bless you, Caroline, for He is Good.*

I hope you have given your heart to Jesus.

With much love,

Your grandmother

"She will be happy to know that you have."

"I hope she knows."

"It's too bad you didn't have these to wear for your own wedding. I'm sorry it took me so long to figure out the safe," Peter apologized.

"No! No, I wouldn't want to wear them. I wore the necklace *you* gave me. Besides, I don't think they're in fashion anymore. I don't really know what to do with them, but I'd like to keep them."

"Keep them in your grandparents' safe," Peter said.

"I suppose. There doesn't seem to be anything of worth, except what was important to my grandmother," summarized Caroline while she returned the items to the safe.

"But isn't that what counts in the long run?" asked Peter. "At least we can paint the wall now!"

※

Caroline jumped into planting a late garden and opening the treehouse her grandfather had built when her uncle was a boy. In his typical style, Grandfather had brought in a crew of workers who turned out an elaborate treehouse on stilts that looked more like a small cottage. Caroline spent long, happy hours cleaning and setting the treehouse to rights after the long winter. She still loved the somewhat idealized mural of the treehouse with its mossy, flower-filled approach that she and Mia had painted on the wall of the back entry. It was a definite improvement to the room Caroline still referred to as her flower room because of her grandmother's collection of lovely vases. The collection now included additional vases which Caroline had arranged to their best advantage in anticipation of many flower arrangements cut from the yard and woods.

   Life settled into a happy time of Peter working a little less and Caroline concentrating on making their home pleasant. She found great contentment in the daily chores of tending the garden, cleaning, cooking, and tackling small projects around the house. When autumn came, she would be ready to go to work wholeheartedly on her master's courses and thesis, but for now she drew every drop of pleasure from the summer that she could. There were rare occasions when Peter had to stay at the university until late, but he made it a priority to eat dinner at home with Caroline unless his presence was absolutely required elsewhere. She dedicated herself to transforming their times together into memorable summer adventures. Dinner was often a barbeque on the small beach at their lake, a picnic in the canoe as they explored every nook and cranny of the shoreline, or a cookout or picnic at the treehouse. Sometimes they paddled over to Grandpa John and Grandma Martha's shore to eat with them or to bring them dinner. Peter sometimes took them out in the canoe or rowboat one at a time since it was becoming more difficult for them to do much rowing on their own.

"I told you we were going to need a bigger rowboat," Peter joked in private to Caroline, a joke that always made them laugh. He had first said it after she accepted his marriage proposal, referring to the time she had slept in the rowboat on the lake and Peter's Grandma and Grandpa had called him with concerns about her safety. Caroline had planned to keep her little adventure private but Peter had driven hours from his doctoral studies to camp on the shore to "protect" her. Caroline, in her rumpled condition, had been both mortified and elated when she discovered him the next morning.

Sundays continued to be a special day set apart for church and they enjoyed Sunday dinners at Peter's parents', out at a restaurant, at Grandma and Grandpa's, or at Caroline and Peter's. They felt so blessed to have such a wonderful home to share with others. Lyndsey and Drew came for the promised lunch one Saturday and enjoyed an extended paddle around the lake, including a stop at the treehouse. Occasionally, they hosted other friends like Mia and Jeff or young couples they were getting to know at church. Matt drove Jo home one weekend and Caroline and Peter loved having them come for dinner.

Of course, the summer passed all too quickly. They consoled themselves with the promise of exploring possible vacation and second honeymoon destinations. Perhaps someday, they would have the time and the money to actually do it! Caroline enjoyed having a dream to pursue, no matter how distant and improbable.

Peter continued to drive his second-hand car because he had paid it off long ago. Caroline continued to drive her grandfather's MG that he had paid cash for when he bought and had it redone in his typical fashion: an over-the-top renovation. But whenever their schedules aligned, or the snow and cold were significant, they rode to the university together in Peter's car. Caroline didn't want Peter to have to spend too much time tinkering with the MG. With his new position, his time was limited. They tried to live as economically as possible. Peter's beginning salary was not large and they felt they needed to be careful, even though they had no mortgage. They felt very fortunate and carefully divided their total income wisely: the first portion, a ten percent tithe, went to the Lord. They made a habit of giving that amount right off the top to their church because they were grateful for the ministry of Pastor Clay and others in their lives and because the church was careful to choose to support other strategic and godly ministries in their own city and around the world.

The next portion of Peter and Caroline's income went to paying all of their monthly bills and required expenses. As the months progressed and they were able to see some progress toward an emergency savings account, they reviewed their budget frequently and were able to add another one percent of income to supporting a needy child through a Christian organization that shared not only needed food, but the Gospel of Jesus' love. Over time, as God blessed their careful giving, they began to feel enabled to designate another percentage of their savings to their future travel. Perhaps in five years, Caroline thought, especially if she was able to find employment after her master's, then they could look seriously at a special honeymoon trip.

So she dreamed of a distant time when things would be more comfortable in terms of income. In the meantime, learning about possible destinations turned out to be an interesting pursuit together. They were on the lookout for travel tips and learning about various cultures. They occasionally watched a travel show, explored information by travel experts online, or checked out a travel show from the library. For Caroline, it was a game that was interesting, something they could do together or on their own in order to share their learning with one another. She never really counted on *doing* any of it. The money her grandparents had left her was gone and, even with discounted tuition, her schooling expenses took a significant part of their income.

They had known it would happen and planned accordingly, but Caroline still felt guilty that Peter was paying for her degree out of his earnings.

Thankfully, her work was not overly demanding that year. She had prepared well for her project and still enjoyed the intense learning necessary to extend it and advance it toward completion. The following summer required Peter to continue teaching a reduced load and Caroline to continue to focus on her degree. They had celebrated their first anniversary quietly at home and took a weekend trip in June between semesters. They knew the upcoming semesters would be more intense for both of them, so they tried to take time throughout the summer whenever they could to be intentionally active outdoors and to do things together.

As always, the summer was over far too soon, leaving many pleasant memories to see them through until the next one. That academic year was busy for both of them. The pressure was on for Caroline to make significant progress toward defending her thesis, and for Peter to continue to develop courses with a new emphasis on partnerships with local businesses to benefit his students. They were both engrossed in things that were important to them.

That Christmas, they hosted the Christmas celebration for Peter's extended family. Caroline thoroughly enjoyed planning special touches to make it a memorable time. They made a list of people to invite, well before Christmas, and drew names for a gift exchange to include everyone who planned to come. Matt agreed to come, which made them all very happy, especially Jo. The week before Christmas, they scheduled an ice skating opportunity for those who wished to participate if the ice was solid, plus a backup walk through the snowy woods and an indoor cookie decorating station for everyone to bring favorite cookies. Guests decorated them to take home, and also left a container behind in the freezer to bring out on Christmas Day. Caroline planned the menu for Christmas dinner, asking specific family members to bring specific dishes, each a specialty of that person and a favorite with everyone. She knew the family traditions by now and made good use of her experience in order to please everyone. It turned out to be a glorious blend of flavors of their favorite well-rounded and more-than-complete Christmas meal.

Before dinner there was a walk down the path to the lake, and after dinner they all retired to a blazing fire in the family room. Caroline had decorated the house to the fullest extent with her grandmother's decorations, the first time she had actually made use of all of them. She filled in with greens from the yard and woods and purchased more candles that brought intimacy and brightness to the large rooms. All in all, she thoroughly enjoyed every bit of the days leading up to Christmas and even the busy day itself. She relished having a family, a real reason for doing all of this! It was rewarding to see everyone enjoy the results. Peter had advised her not to overdo it, to keep it simple, but she was happy, so happy, that she had done everything she could think of to make it the best Christmas ever. And when the departing guests asserted that they knew where to hold the family Christmas celebration from now on, she didn't mind at all.

CHAPTER SEVEN

The Christian leadership team met at their house to outline the rest of the school year. Caroline had taken on an advisory role. They always met around the time of her birthday, and this time it was the week after. They'd had a great time reviewing the events of the fall and rejoicing over the five decisions for Christ at Christmas time. Caroline was discipling the three girls and Josh's successor was discipling the two young men who had accepted Christ. Peter helped them focus their efforts for the remainder of the year and especially for the movie event coming up. He would participate in a panel discussion they had arranged with an unbelieving professor. They would continue to pray that Peter's overt Christian witness was something acceptable to the administration.

He was doing his utmost to connect companies with good, solid workers, and was busy setting up his second annual job fair at the university. Caroline was excited about this new area of growth for the Computer Science majors and had committed to making brownies and snacks for the job fair. After all, it was Peter's effort that had landed her an internship for the summer.

Peter and Caroline tried to make their second anniversary as special as possible with a return to the château-like restaurant that Peter had once taken Caroline to. Before they left home, Peter surprised her with a walk to the boathouse that suddenly had acquired a new, larger, and sleeker rowboat!

"Peter!" Caroline exclaimed when she saw it, "I didn't think you were serious about the bigger boat!"

"Of course I was! Well, maybe not at first, but I was beginning to wonder if the old one was going to spring a leak on us and strand us in the middle of the lake."

"That would not be good," she laughingly agreed. "I can't wait for summer! But I'll never be able to handle it myself."

"I think once it's in the water, you'll find it easier to row than the old one. We'll keep the old one and hire Lyndsey and Drew to make it over, that is if they will condescend to work on such a lowly thing. Anyway, I'd rather not worry about you being on the lake alone this summer during those times when I can't be with you. I'm going to be pretty swamped this summer.

"Swamped! Ha! Get it?" Peter grinned.

"I get it. I'm going to be pretty swamped myself with a fulltime internship. Thank you." She stretched high enough to give him a kiss on the cheek. "I hope we both get a chance to use the new one. By the way, Matt's driving Jo home for Easter so maybe they'll have time to come over. We're all invited to your parents' for Easter dinner."

"Okay. Sounds good!"

On Easter Sunday, the church was filled with white lilies. The message that Pastor Clay preached came straight from Scripture, the music moved Caroline to tears, and the service concluded with Pastor Clay shouting, "He is risen!" and the congregation responding, "He is risen indeed!" with increasing intensity each time. The organ burst into a magnificent "Christ the Lord is risen today! Hallelujah!" as they made their way out.

At Peter's parents' house, everyone was seated at the table when his father, Brett, stood to ask the Lord's blessing on the food; but instead of beginning, he nodded at Matt and said, "I believe Matt has something he would like to say."

Caroline held her breath as he began. "I want you all to know that I have asked Jo to be my wife and she has graciously, perhaps foolishly, accepted my proposal and I couldn't be happier!"

Amid the exclamations and clapping, he knelt next to Jo and presented a ring that surprised even Jo.

"Oh, it's lovely, Matt! I didn't expect such a beautiful ring!"

Caroline could hardly contain herself. She sat across from them, stunned, but managed to cheer with everyone else.

121

Then Jo had to exhibit the ring to the table in general and eventually Father was able to explain that he and Mother had been blessed with the news earlier and had given their happy consent and blessing to Matt and Jo. Of course, Peter and Caroline couldn't stay in their seats, and jumped up to hug them and welcome Matt into the family.

"So, let's pray before everything gets even colder," Brett attempted again, once they were all back in their seats.

"Oh, it's all staying warm in the kitchen!" Claire assured them all.

Eventually, Brett had his way and took the opportunity to pray on behalf of all of them for God's blessings to be poured out on their daughter and Matt before asking God to bless the food and their time together on this special Easter. "And thank you, most of all, Jesus, for giving yourself as a sacrifice. For taking on our sins and offering God's forgiveness in their place, we are grateful. We pray all these things in your precious name, Jesus. Amen."

Everyone echoed the "Amen" and looked up with joy and anticipation of further explanations of Jo and Matt's story along with the feast soon to be placed before them. It was a truly special Easter.

Jo and Matt came to Peter and Caroline's the next evening and the four of them watched *The Mission* together. It was so moving that for the rest of her life, whenever Caroline heard the music of *Gabriel's Oboe*, tears were inevitable. The movie plot was especially meaningful to them: Matt and Jo intended to go as missionaries to a place where the gospel was unknown. When the movie ended, they sat in silence, stunned by the ending, each knowing without speaking that both Jo and Matt were prepared to give their lives if necessary in order to take the story of God's love to those who had never heard, but they were stunned by the injustice of the movie. Their thoughts covered a variety of perspectives.

Jo was thankful her parents had not seen the movie. She knew her parents were aware of the potential dangers of mission work, but she wasn't sure her mother would be able to see her young daughter in the role of a martyr. From then on, Jo prayed that she and Matt, along with all of their families, would be prepared by God for whatever lay ahead of them. Matt inwardly humbled himself before God and prayed for protection and provision for his promised wife and that he would have the wisdom not to lead her into harmful situations. Peter and Caroline began to pray for God's guidance, blessings, and protection for Jo and Matt throughout their lives.

Peter eventually managed to span the silence by voicing a prayer for God to bless and use Matt and Jo to bring the gospel to the places and people groups God knew would be responsive to the good news of the gospel, and that God would prepare them for carrying out the mission he had for them. Jo always felt it was that moment that was the real beginning of their preparation for ministry, regardless of all the seminary learning that they had completed.

    Caroline defended her thesis in May, followed by a graduation that truly celebrated her long, intense time as a student at the university. It wasn't easy to let go, now that Peter was there permanently, but she was excited about her internship for a think tank, which would hopefully lead to a full-time job offer. It was fun to tackle the problems her job posed in her specialty of artificial intelligence. She was consumed with trying to think of ways that artificial intelligence could lead to artificial general intelligence. If a computer could learn to do certain things better than humans, then could they develop a system with general or broad enough learning that it could accomplish just about anything? Could it truly learn? Could it accomplish any task in a fraction of the time it would take a whole team of people, no matter what was asked of it?

    That summer seemed to fly by. With Caroline and Peter both working, the demands on the two of them were immense. Peter surprised her by bringing home eight climbing roses to plant around the gazebo because she had mentioned how nice the pink blossoms would look arching over the openings. She watched their progress, glad to have something to look forward to, and took every opportunity to train the growing canes to the shape of the gazebo. They had decided to have the lawn company do more, so that they had less to do. It was worth it.

The fall brought the job offer Caroline was hoping for: she was so happy that she wouldn't have to do a job search and potentially refocus her thoughts and efforts on another, less interesting, aspect of artificial intelligence.

The greatest event of that autumn was Jo and Matt's wedding. Caroline did everything she could to help Jo and Claire plan the event. It was easy to remember all of the wonderful things Jo had done for her, so she tried to do the same for Jo. The entire family was involved as much as possible and it gave them all a truly joyous reason to celebrate. Jo and Matt had one more year of seminary after their wedding, and with everyone busily back at work and school, the months began to roll by.

Caroline stared at the June airline tickets to Paris in disbelief. It was their third anniversary and *this* was Peter's gift to her? She was going to Paris? She blinked and looked up at Peter.

"Peter! This is too much! Can we afford this?"

"It's okay. We can! I told you we would someday! We can't let all of that travel research go to waste."

"But someday is different than this summer. Are you sure we should do this? Can we really do this?"

"Probably not if your grandparents hadn't left you a house to inherit. We've had an unusual financial boost at the beginning of our marriage. It's quite an advantage and allows us to spend quite a lot on helping others, but I wanted to do something special for *you*. You've been working hard, and I don't think we should wait another year. I want you to know that I notice all the little things you do for me in addition to all the things you have on your plate."

"But Peter, you do so much for me. Shouldn't we use this kind of money for something more worthwhile?"

"Pardon me, but *I* think spending it on making you happy is a very worthwhile cause. Besides, we'll be making memories together. Shared memories are valuable. Once we start our family, we won't be able to do things like this. Just the fact that we'll both have three weeks off this year seems extraordinary. I think we should go!"

"True, but I just never thought I would be able to even think about going to Paris yet!"

"Is there a place you'd rather go? I don't think I can change it at this point. I chose Paris because of things you've said when we talk about traveling. But we can always add your *best* dream destination to our list for the future."

"No, Paris is fine! I can't think of anything better." She looked at the tickets again. "I'm going to Paris? We're going to Paris!"

Peter laughed. He was enjoying her stunned reaction.

"Wow!" she exclaimed as she studied the dates. "Fifteen days in June? That's a long time to pay for a hotel in Paris!"

"I was thinking we wouldn't have to stay in Paris the entire time. We can use it as our beginning point and fly out of there to return home, but there are some other sights I'd like to see outside of Paris."

"That's a great idea. What would you most like to see?"

"I thought I'd let you choose the sights in Paris. I'm interested in the Louvre and a couple of other things there, but I'd really like to try to get to the town of Chartres to see the cathedral."

"Is that where the stained glass windows are that you were telling me about?"

"Yes. I want to see them for myself. They must be quite extraordinary."

"That sounds great!" Caroline assented, already trying to decide how to prioritize the possibilities in Paris. She began to research the famous sites in Paris whenever she had a spare moment, becoming familiar with the online map of the city. She and Peter looked at a variety of hotels and settled on a moderately-priced (for Paris) small hotel. They made the hotel reservation as soon as possible, thankful to have found a room available for the time they would be in the city. The nearest underground Metro stop was a short walk away. They soon realized that the Paris Pass would give them entrance to many of the tourist sites, and they carefully chose the passes that would be of the most use to them. Realizing that the hop-on, hop-off bus would be their best transportation from site to site, they purchased a pass for their time frame. It felt like they were spending a lot of money before even getting to Paris, but they were hopeful it would save them money, time, and frustration once there. Caroline wanted to maximize the time they had there, so planning ahead as much as possible seemed the best way to see the particular places that interested them. As soon as they had the assurance of transportation, and the routes the bus followed, she was able to reserve museum passes. Some were timed admissions, so she and Peter made educated guesses about transportation times and the length of time needed to see what they wanted at each museum. Having to be so detailed with everything scheduled on vacation seemed so restricting, but it also seemed to be the only way to see the things they thought they would be particularly disappointed not to see.

CHAPTER EIGHT

They had decided to splurge on a taxi from the airport to their hotel because they knew they would arrive fatigued from the flight and the hotel was a little distance from the nearest Metro stop. They were glad they had made that decision. It was an interesting ride through the city to the narrow street with its row of small hotels on the quaint Île Saint-Louis, an island in the Seine River. The taxi ride helped them orient themselves as they spotted points along the way that they recognized from maps and their online research.

The next morning, they turned down the immense tray of breads that was supposed to represent breakfast and managed to order eggs and juice. A walk to the Metro and a walk after the Metro finally got them to their hop-on, hop-off bus passes. They were off!

It was a strange feeling to be driving up the famous street called the Champs-Élysées. They got out at the Place de l'Étoile and began the long climb up the inside of Napoleon's Arc de Triomphe. They counted the claustrophobic steps, and the feeling didn't go away when they emerged into a room just short of the top. The ceiling was high, a barrel vault over the entire room, but it seemed low, perhaps because there was little daylight. It felt like a bunker. It was a relief to be able to walk around and they managed to learn quite a lot from the displays; but it wasn't until they climbed a few more steps to emerge on top and into the open air, that they realized how high they were above the city. Suspended above the center of a great wheel of streets, the greatest of which was the broad and beautiful Champs-Élysées, they easily spotted many of the sights on their To See list. But straight down the Champs-Élysées, lost in the distance, was the Louvre. Tomorrow.

The Louvre was the Louvre. It seemed to go on forever! They browsed through the left wing, taking pictures of ancient bronze pillars and spectacular winged bulls from Assyria that dwarfed them, and on through the end of the U-shaped buildings.

Eventually, they came upon a room with pictures of the process of restoring the Winged Victory. It took them a minute to realize that the model displayed was not the real Winged Victory, which was a great relief because it just wasn't that impressive. Indeed, when they rounded the corner and saw the real thing, in all its glory, they were properly impressed with its size. They went to the bottom of the stairs, just to see it at the top, and took more pictures.

At lunch time, they proceeded through the right hand

wing, or Denon Building, and upstairs to the café to stand in line. When it was their turn, they asked to be seated on the terrace outside. For some reason, there were only a few tables outside, enjoying the view over the glass pyramid and the courtyard, across to the left wing of the building. They were so glad to be seated outdoors, and the view was priceless! To the left, the Tuileries gardens stretched out of sight. They were exhausted and spent some time resting there, in the shade high above the press of the crowds. Then, thinking they would take in the Mona Lisa, they worked their way back to the room reserved for the picture. As they approached, they could hardly get to the doorway of the room, but when they managed to look in the room and see the number of people mashed in front of the picture, all with cell phones raised, they decided they would not join the crowd. The picture was clearly visible above their heads.

"We've seen it!" said Peter.

"I agree! Let's get out of here."

They managed to see a few other things before leaving the building and then spent some time walking in the park-like Tuileries.

"Wow! That was crazy!" Peter said, referring to the Mona Lisa crowd.

"I'll say!" Caroline agreed. "They were all just taking a picture of it so they could say they had seen it. I didn't expect so many people. I thought it would be more like a typical museum with a room and some benches to sit and contemplate the picture."

"Who would guess there would be so many people? And throughout all of the building, especially after lunch."

It was a warm day, and they decided to take the Metro back to the area of their hotel. They came up from the Metro station and walked across the Pont Marie bridge to their home away from home on the Île Saint-Louis. After resting a bit in their air conditioned room, they made their way over another bridge to the Île de la Cité, an adjoining island, amazed at the work progressing on Notre Dame, and found the Flower Market. It was too bad that the cathedral was closed, but the devastation caused by the fire would take some time to repair. They found the Flower Market very restful and interesting and passed on many temping purchases that would make their room special but would have to be left in Paris. After the Flower Market, they found Sainte Chapelle, where they had a skip-the-line timed reservation for the next morning.

On the way back to their hotel, being famished, they stopped for dinner at a sidewalk café and endured the long, unhurried French meal. First, they were brought one course, and much later the remainder of the meal. The waiter disappeared both times, so they enjoyed what they had to eat and drink and chatted about what they'd seen so far. They had trouble getting the bill when they decided it really was time to go, but eventually, they succeeded in paying for the meal and strolled back to their hotel. It was an easy decision to call it a day!

The next morning, they lined up for the Sainte Chapelle skip-the-line tour and discovered that their skip-the-line didn't really mean skip-the-line, so they waited in line with everyone else. Evidently no one was skipping the line at the moment. It was worth the wait. As they entered the lower chapel, Caroline experienced a sense of disappointment. Where were the stained glass windows? They wandered around the small room, listening to the self-guided tour until they figured out where the tiny spiral staircase was that led upstairs. Here, were the magnificent windows! The entire room was made of soaring stained glass windows, with very little space between windows. It was magnificent! They listened to the tour explaining the history of the building, the windows, the Rose Window, and the famous relics such as the Crown of Thorns. It was supposedly, though unrealistically, the real Crown of Thorns that had adorned Christ's head at the crucifixion and that had once been stored here for the king to appreciate. Of course, all this grandeur and religion was intended only for the king. The rest of the population got the plain, dark room underneath Sainte Chapelle. How sad that an entire country had been lost to secularism as a result of elitist control. After just standing, trying to absorb the experience, they emerged from Sainte Chapelle satiated with light and color and form, and made their way to a small, open café to mull over what it all meant.

That evening they returned to Sainte Chapelle for a concert, enjoyed reading about Sainte Chapelle's history, and then found their way to a nearby sidewalk café, where they noticed the performers had congregated. The food was good, and they thanked the performers for their excellence before leaving.

The next day, they set out to find the Musée de Cluny, but had some trouble finding it because the bus didn't go all the way to the museum. After setting out on foot and asking directions several times, they approached the building from the back; but managed to make their way to the front of the building where they were happy to enter through the visitors' entrance and proceed through the Roman baths. Persevering, they finally found the Old Testament kings' heads that had been cut off the Notre Dame statues by over-zealous revolutionaries. The original heads of the kings of Israel and Judah had formed a line above the entrance to Notre Dame but, during the French Revolution, they had lost their heads along with Louis XVI and Marie Antoinette! The heads were found buried in a back yard much later, in 1977, after they had already been replaced by perfectly natural looking heads.

"They *look* like they've been buried for years," remarked Peter, referring to their worn appearance and to many that were missing their noses.

"It obviously would not have been a good idea to place them back on the bodies!" Caroline agreed, wondered again at the blood-thirsty revolution that had left France a secular state. Perhaps it was, in reality, a secular state long before the revolution, with pathetic kings propping up their egos, reigns, and coffers with claims of God's approval. Was that taking God's name in vain?

They enjoyed the progression of artifacts from the Roman Empire, through the early middle ages, the Romanesque era, and the Gothic era. They remarked over the beauty of early stained glass, but when they came to the Lady and the Unicorn tapestries, they were entranced. Reading the story of each tapestry was fascinating, and they spent time before each one, observing the details of flora and fauna and trying to connect what was happening with the particular sense (smell, touch, etc.) allegedly depicted. What was the sixth tapestry all about? Something sensual, no doubt, but Caroline loved the foxes, rabbits, and other small creatures adorning some of the tapestries and the plants. She liked some of the tamer color schemes and wondered if anyone had done replicas but decided she really wouldn't want them in her home after all. There was something uncomfortably mysterious about their existence.

In the morning, they boarded the hop-on, hop-off bus to the Musée d'Orsay, a former train station on the left bank of the Seine. This museum was crowded, but very open and light and airy so that the crowds seemed dwarfed by the high, barreled ceiling. The clocks, so beautifully portrayed in the movie about the orphan boy, Hugo, gave some hint as to what the building had been before it was turned into a museum. The former train station sported two fifteen-foot-tall (they estimated) clock faces that faced the River Seine to the north. When they walked up to one of them, they could see straight through it, to another magnificent view of the city.

"Look, there's the Church of the Sacred Heart!" Peter pointed out. Sure enough, looking through the clock, Caroline could see Sacré-Cœur in the distance, all the way across the city, standing prominently on the top of Montmartre.

They enjoyed the impressionist paintings, the magnificent sculptures, the decorative arts, and their break for lunch in the beauty of the surroundings. Such a beautiful spot for a café!

They spent another day doing the Eiffel Tower justice, managing not to buy a miniature Eiffel Tower from a variety of hucksters' blankets spread on the ground. The view, of course, astounded. That night they used their Paris Pass for a boat ride down the Seine and back as the sun set. If they could have gotten off the boat, they could have been back to their hotel in minutes, but later that night they had to get a taxi back to their hotel because the boat ride kept them out so late they missed the last bus! The Eiffel Tower and the evening boat ride, they agreed, had been too much for one day.

They spent a day at the Musée de l'Orangerie, standing in line again for what seemed a long time in the heat and then gratefully absorbing the cool peace and tranquility of Monet's water lilies in different seasons and different lighting. Reading about the history of the museum was fascinating! Monet himself had put the enormous paintings in place. Caroline and Peter were especially excited to be going to Monet's home and gardens outside of Paris when they left the city in a few days.

The next day, they took the Metro to the stop for Sacré-Cœur, the Sacred Heart Church. They emerged at the bottom of a steep hill where they were a bit bemused by the tourist attractions. People thronged up the street; there would have been no room for cars. In the street were hucksters of all kinds. Both sides of the street were lined with touristy shops full of T-shirts, scarves, hats, post cards, and keepsakes of Paris. They stopped at one that had hats for sale on a rack outside the shop, and chose an inexpensive, white one made of paper for Caroline to wear. It looked just like white straw, and in no way would have suggested to anyone that it was made of paper! She was thankful for it, as it was a hot day. They made their way up the street, continually amused that anyone would pay to play the shell game in the street. More than once, they saw the proprietor of a blanket shuffling walnut shells to confuse and confound the tourists. How amazing that anyone would pay to play such an obvious deception!

Eventually, they made their way to the funicular and were

deposited at the bottom of a very wide and very tall staircase that circled the hill in front of the church. When they reached the Sacred Heart church, they sat in the sanctuary, observing the brilliantly colored mosaic of Christ standing with outstretched hands and a heart glowing with love for the world. Eventually, they somehow became part of the crowd shuffling slowly clockwise around the interior perimeter of the church. Caroline sighed and wondered why they were there. *Lord, I don't feel very well. It's so hot! Please help me get through this!* Looking up through an arched opening she saw the immense curving mural of Jesus smiling down at *her*. It shocked her and made her happy, as though he had personally heard and answered her prayer. She nudged Peter and pointed up, smiling. When they came around to a place where they could see more of the figure, Christ's heart of love for the world was clearly displayed, there in his chest. Caroline reminded herself that she needed to keep her heart warmed to the needs of the world.

 Their time in Paris drew to a close, so the next morning they walked their suitcases to the Metro, headed out of town, and connected to a train to get out of the city. When they arrived in the town near Claude Monet's home, they picked up a rental car, stowed their suitcases, and drove, finding their way to the home of Monet. Caroline loved their tickets which had photos of the house and gardens that made them look like impressionist paintings. The house was long and pink with bright green trim and shutters. Monet had added to each end of the house, making an attractive family home. And the gardens! Caroline had never seen such a wealth of flowers. They were so thickly planted that there were no spaces between the gorgeous, prolific blooms. It was truly incredible.

They found the rather prosaic tunnel under the road that emerged at one end of the lily pond and stood on the Japanese bridge, looking at the tourists on the Japanese bridge at the other end. It was hard at first to focus on the pond and the lily pads, but the more they did, as they walked around the pond, the more they became interested in how Monet painted them, time and time again. They stood on the other bridge and looked back at the entrance end, they explored all of the little side paths, and then headed back to the gardens.

When they entered the house with their timed ticket, they saw his study, other quaint rooms, a brilliant yellow dining room, and a clean blue and white kitchen that made them both happy. What a wonderful house!

CHAPTER NINE

"This must be it," Caroline said. A small, unobtrusive sign on a low rock wall was the only confirmation that they had arrived at the country bed and breakfast where they had reserved a room. The narrow but adequate gravel drive led directly to a two-story building that was large but modest in appearance. The atmosphere surrounding the home was more farmlike than grand. No formal gardens were in sight as they drove nearly to the door and stopped. Before they could emerge from the car, a man and woman stepped out of the oversized but simple front door. Caroline and Peter knew the couple were originally from India and had come to know Jesus through the witness of friends. Peter had spoken to the owners on the phone, telling them how excited they were to find believers offering their home as a B and B, so they already knew how much Caroline and Peter appreciated their faith.

"Welcome!" The middle-aged couple introduced themselves using only first names and English that was very British sounding. "You must be Peter and Caroline. We are so happy to meet you!" exclaimed Ananya, the woman. "Come in! Come in!"

"I'll get your luggage," Faraj said, ushering them through the door.

Caroline immediately felt at home with the couple. They were dressed simply and practically in their native garb. They seemed very down to earth and at home here themselves, an impression that was strengthened as the wife showed them through the first floor. Though the rooms were large the décor was simple and homey.

Their hostess began the tour of the ground floor, "When we purchased it, the structure was sound but it had been vacant for some time. We were very fortunate that it was basically still intact, but it had been used as storage on a farm and there was a lot of clearing out to be done. We were able to do that fairly quickly and once the repairs were made we had a relatively blank slate. We did all of the work ourselves from that point on."

Caroline complimented her on the work they had done. "It looks wonderful!" The last room their hostess led them to was the dining room.

"This is where we serve breakfast, anytime between seven and nine in the morning. I have a choice of two specialty dishes each day. "

"That sounds lovely," Caroline commented, noticing that the room was simple and elegant though far from stately. She loved the two-toned stone floor beneath their feet. Each square of smoothly worn stone contained a fleur-de-lis design embedded in the center. The beautiful, but again unpretentious, floor gave her a sense that the home had lasted through the long and obscure history of its use, thus preserving the original dignity of the building.

The timeless flooring continued, leading them back to the foyer where their host stood waiting for them, suitcases in hand.

"This way," he said, motioning them toward the comfortably-worn stone stairway. Caroline again felt grateful for the enduring stone that seemed to belong to the building, validating the work it had taken to restore the usefulness of the structure. Its worn but elegant nature stated to her that the "château" had been a true home and was once again what it was intended to be; not a grand château, but a country home that had survived from more prosperous times.

"We have given you the suite," Faraj stated, leading the way down the short hallway to a door. He placed a suitcase on the floor and opened the door, indicating that they should enter the spacious room. To their right a window seat framed a bay window overlooking the front yard. The bed was to the left. Their host placed the suitcases by a set of doors they assumed was a closet and showed them the hallway that led to a bathroom on the right and also to a flight of stairs straight ahead.

"This is yours to use as a sitting room," he said with pride, motioning them upwards. "We added it just last year."

Peter and Caroline were astounded to emerge from the stairway into a glassed solarium flooded with light and broad views. From the back of what Americans called the third floor, they looked across surrounding fields with suggestions here and there of distant farm buildings or the occasional village.

"This is quite amazing!" Peter exclaimed. "Did you do the work yourselves?"

"No, I have to admit that we had a builder, but we came up with the idea and worked with an architect to design it."

"I love it!" Caroline said, mesmerized by the view.

"Well done," commented Peter. He didn't want Faraj and his wife to feel insulted because he had assumed the work had been done by them. "It was certainly worth it."

"I'm glad you like it."

When they were alone, Caroline and Peter hung their clothing in the closet and checked out the view from the bay window before gravitating to their sitting room.

"Where could we add one of these to our house?" Caroline murmured softly, absorbing the view.

Peter laughed. "It does remind me of your grandmother's study upstairs."

"Yes, I think you're right. Maybe we could finish more of the attic and do something like this."

"I don't think I'm quite up for that," Peter said with a frown.

"We'll put it on our 'Someday' list," Caroline said dreamily.

"I'm in trouble if all the elegance and grandeur of Paris is giving you ideas!"

Caroline laughed. "This place is just what we need after all of our sightseeing. The slower pace, the countryside. It's a great place for us to relax and rest. I think it's just what we need right now."

"It is restful," Peter agreed.

They spent some time settling in and exploring their suite before responding to their hosts' earlier invitation to join them for a snack downstairs. It was fascinating to hear their story of how God had intervened in their behalf to deliver them from threats and persecution. The couple expressed continually how grateful they were for all that they had.

Peter and Caroline eventually found themselves back in the glass enclosed sitting room with books in their hands, eyes roaming the countryside. Later, they asked their hosts where to go for dinner and followed their directions to a small local restaurant. After a very leisurely French meal they took a drive around the area before returning to the château. They explored the grounds, as they had been invited to do anytime, and rejoiced over the farm buildings, the stone walls surrounding the yard, and the flowers. They were surprised to discover the chickens in a large chicken wire enclosure adjacent to one of the small barns, and sheep enclosed in a pen that opened onto the field behind the house. The gate was, in fact, standing open but the sheep gathered eagerly around a manger, apparently waiting for grain or some other feed. It all seemed comfortably rural and homey but well kept, and informally but neatly manicured. Spending the rest of the evening in the sitting room observing the changes in the sky as the sun was setting was pleasant: it was private and cozy but completely, quietly entertaining.

Breakfast the next morning was served in the dining room with lovely dishes, yet it seemed very informal with their hostess pressing them to enjoy the fresh fruit cups and omelets with homemade preserves on excellent toast. They began with juice and delicious fresh fruit in stemware and enjoyed meeting the other couple currently staying in the house. Eager to see the countryside, Peter and Caroline listened with interest to descriptions of the places the couple had seen over the last few days. Armed with information from them and their host and hostess they had a great day of sightseeing and enjoyed lunch at a local riverside restaurant.

Two more days of similar experiences, including one very meaningful stop at the beach at Normandy, filled them with satisfaction over their choice of accommodations and the surrounding area. It was with regret that they said goodbye and began the drive south to their next stop, closer to the Loire River Valley.

"If I wasn't so curious about the second place we've

reserved, I'd be content to just stay here." Caroline commented as they drove away. "But our next stop must be much larger and fancier than the first place. It's amazing how many centuries the château has been passed down in this family. The owners must be wealthy to have such a beautiful place. You wonder why they run a B and B. I wonder if we'll see much of them."

"Maybe not. They probably have their own private wing."

"I suppose."

Their next home away from home was buried deeper in the countryside than the last and surrounded by open land, but as they approached the setting and the château itself, the impression was less agricultural than their previous location. The château was a large structure, older perhaps, but very solid. Not exactly grand, but representing a simple, unadorned elegance in stone. Much more elegant than their last accommodations. How was it that it still seemed so informal here? Even the front door seemed unostentatious, as were the owners who issued from it, introducing themselves and welcoming Peter and Caroline with energy and warmth.

Inside, the grand sweep of the stone stairway led to dim and mysterious areas above the entry.

"This is our office area," the husband commented before they ascended, indicating an open door at the end of the hallway, under the stairway. We are often to be found here, so please come in anytime. After you are settled in your room,

147

we would be happy to give you a tour of the house and grounds."

The beautiful rose-colored bedroom overlooked the front gardens, and their host and hostess opened the generous double windows wide. With the typical European lack of screens, the view was broad yet intimate and Caroline was captivated by the scene of a little girl playing with a large dog on the grass below. She couldn't help but exclaim about the beauty of the room and the view. She and Peter both thanked their host and hostess and promised to join them soon for a tour.

"They're so nice!" Caroline commented once the door was closed.

"Not what I expected," Peter agreed.

They took a few minutes to unpack and freshen up before finding their way down the immense stairway. It was all so beautiful!

The "office" was prefaced by an elegant sitting room where they were invited to sit on a comfortably overstuffed sofa. Their host and hostess asked about their trip and after a few minutes, the owners began the tour, just for them, explaining some of the history of the building as they went from room to room. They had restored much of the building and the furnishings that were no doubt costly antiques yet still used by the family and guests. Their hosts emphasized that they were to feel at home.

Peter and Caroline were again directed to a local restaurant for dinner. They took a scenic route back after dinner and were once again warmly greeted by the owners. Caroline found herself immensely enjoying their perfect English spoken with a truly elegant French accent. They spent quite some time recommending which of the famous châteaux and other sites were within driving distance and would be of interest in particular to Peter and Caroline, based on their interests and their few remaining days.

"Do you have any interest in nearby cathedrals?" the husband asked.

"Yes," Peter replied. In fact we have reserved a tour at Chartres for the day after tomorrow."

"Splendid! You will discover amazing things about the stained glass there if you are on the tour."

"Yes. I look forward to it! I have read a little about them. They sound amazing."

"Be sure to stop in the gift shop and buy the books about the windows before you leave. They are worth their weight in gold."

"We have a chef who comes in to serve our guests breakfast," the wife said as they prepared to ascend the magnificent stairway, "so just come to the solarium between eight and nine in the morning. He will let you know what is on the menu each day. He can prepare picnic lunches to take with you on your excursions if you let him know the day before. On Friday, he is serving an optional dinner for our guests. I believe it is roast leg of lamb with fresh vegetables from his garden. He lives in the nearby village. You probably drove through it on your way here."

The tour was fascinating, simply because centuries of existing records revealed the history of the family and the property. Because of the farm records, they even knew when the impressive farm buildings and various parts of the house had been built or refurbished. When Caroline asked how the house escaped the French Revolution and both world wars, the host replied that it was a small, inconsequential place buried in the French countryside. Fortunately, no one wanted it.

Caroline and Peter were anxious to see a real, tourist-type château, so drove to Cheverny the next day and enjoyed the references to Tin Tin and the entire cast of the computer animated movie, with humorous Captain Haddock's home itself based on the beautiful house at Cheverny. They wandered around the gorgeous grounds, saw the feeding of the hounds at the appointed time (Such well-mannered but loud hounds!), and made their way through the gardens which surrounded an island of colorful orchids continually sprayed by fine mists. They enjoyed lunch and ice cream in the Cheverny Café de l'Orangerie before heading for their home away from home.

The next day, they drove a longer distance back toward Paris, to Chartres Cathedral, which topped a high hill in the middle of the town. They drove as close as they could get and parked on the street, running up the hill to get to their tour appointment on time.

As they sat, looking up at the three windows on the west end of the cathedral, and listening to their guide, they were interested in the windows and what he had to say about them.

"From down here, we lose some perspective. How big do you think they are?" he asked his audience. Caroline looked up at the windows, judging each square to be about 16 to 18 inches across. After giving them a few minutes to think, he added, "In this particular window in the center, which depicts the incarnation of Christ, each of those squares is four *feet* by four *feet*. As you can see, this window is three squares wide and ten squares tall, plus the border all around." Caroline was amazed! Each window was more than twelve feet wide and much taller! She'd had no idea they were so large.

Their guide went on to explain that the reason for the windows and statuary was to teach the common people biblical information in the twelfth and thirteenth centuries. Few were able to read scripture for themselves, so they had to rely on stained glass that told the stories of the Bible, and on statues of Old Testament kings, prophets and other prominent people.

❧ CHAPTER TEN ☙

"Take a look at the window on the right. What do you see at the bottom? This window dates from about A.D. 1150. You see a man, reclining, with a tree growing from his stomach. This is Jesse, the father of David, from whom Isaiah foretold, 'And there shall come forth a rod out of the stem of Jesse, and a branch shall grow out of his roots.' As you follow the tree up the window, you see from Jessie's groin the kings are growing, most likely David, Solomon, Roboam, and Abia. Mary, rather than Joseph, is the next figure, being the means of the incarnation, and the last figure at the top, is Christ. At each side, all the way up, are Old Testament prophets carrying scrolls with their names on them, but it is the figure at the top that demands our attention. Jesus, the fulfillment of the prophecy.

"The window in the center is called the Incarnation Window." Their guide continued to explain the window from left to right, bottom to top, some squares depicting the annunciation, the visitation, the nativity with the babe not placed in the manger but sacramentally upon an altar, the annunciation to the shepherds, the adoration of the magi, the presentation in the temple, the massacre of the holy innocents (Herod's order to kill the young male children of Bethlehem), the flight into Egypt, Joseph's dream, the baptism of Jesus, the entry of Jesus into Jerusalem, and (true to Catholic tradition) Mary enthroned at the top.

"The window on the left is called the Passion and Resurrection Window," the guide continued. He continued to explain the panels depicting the Passion Week, the crucifixion, and the resurrection, followed by Christ's appearances to various people the following week.

Peter and Caroline followed their guide from window to window, more and more amazed at the theology so clearly presenting the story of the downfall of mankind, the promised One, the birth of Jesus, and the glorious hope of his return and eternal reign.

Another window they particularly enjoyed was called the Good Samaritan and Adam and Eve Window. Starting at the bottom, the window showed Jesus telling the parable of the Good Samaritan while the top depicted the creation by God of Adam and then Eve, the eating of the forbidden fruit in the Garden of Eden, and the expulsion from the garden followed by the sin of Cain in killing his brother Abel. Why were the stories of Adam and Eve paired with the Good Samaritan parable? The connection was due to the interpretation of the Good Samaritan parable in the Middle Ages. In the parable, the man leaving Jerusalem represented Adam and Eve leaving the garden after the fall. The attack by robbers represented Satan attacking us and leaving us helpless. The priest and the Levite represented the failure of the Old Testament Law to redeem. The Good Samaritan represented Jesus who came to save us, to to bind up our wounds, and to pay our debt, with the promise to return.

"How beautiful! I didn't know that," Caroline whispered to Peter.

"I've never heard that interpretation of the Good Samaritan," said Peter. "It seems I have missed out, but it certainly makes sense!"

At the end of the tour, they thanked their guide profusely and headed to the gift shop only to discover their guide's name on numerous books explaining the cathedral's history and architecture. He was actually quite famous for his life's work! They purchased a book in the gift shop that they knew wasn't available online.

"Look," Peter pointed out. "We can get these other ones after we get home so we don't have to pack so many heavy books."

Caroline reluctantly placed the book she was looking at back on the rack, realizing that what Peter had said was true. They would definitely be purchasing more once they were home.

In the car on the way back to the château, they discussed

each of the windows they had seen and the statuary of the exterior, rejoicing in the surety of the age-old story of redemption.

They had enjoyed every moment of their French vacation, but Caroline was glad that it was time to return home. The flight across the ocean was long, followed by a long lay-over to catch their flight home. Peter's parents picked them up at the airport and dropped them at home without coming in. They left their suitcases unopened, showered, and dropped into bed. It was good to be home.

Thankfully, they had a few days to recover before their vacation was over. It was great fun distributing the gifts they had bought for Peter's mom and dad, Grandpa and Grandma Lockwood, Jo and Matt, and even Grandpa and Grandma Larson. Soon enough, they were back at work, and the weeks began to roll by, but they often laughed over memories of attempted French language and the eccentricities of French waiters. They had many shared memories of Paris, the French countryside, and the châteaux they had visited. Caroline felt a growing conviction that the French people in general needed the gospel. Peter wondered what they could do to minister to the French people and turned over short-term mission possibilities in his head. It wouldn't be soon, he knew, with Caroline's job and his teaching commitments. Perhaps someday.

EPILOG

Where did that truck come from? Lord, help me! Caroline felt crushing pain beyond anything she had ever experienced and then nothing.

"We're going to operate. Miss, can you hear me? We can't guarantee the baby will survive. Do you want to abort the baby or do you want us to try to save it? You're seriously injured. Do you understand?"

"Don't take the baby," Caroline whispered.

The surgeon leaned closer. "We can concentrate on saving you if we take the baby."

"No! Don't harm baby!"

"You understand that we may lose both of you."

Oh, God! Don't let them harm the baby. "Save baby."

"You want us to save the baby?"

"Yes"

"You heard the lady," the surgeon said, straightening up. "Let's get to work."

God, please save Peter's baby! Don't let them harm the baby.

※

Caroline was in the deepest agony. She could never have imagined a person could be in such pain. From the depth of a well of pain, she spoke to God. *Why, God? Why must I suffer so?*

Her spirit was directed to the cross hanging above the door to her hospital room. The room was dark and her eyes were closed, but she could easily picture it because she had appreciated it when she first noticed it.

"You are sharing in the sufferings of Christ."

She recoiled from the thought. She was not worthy to share in his sufferings on the cross. How much more he had endured! What he had accomplished! Who he was!

Yet there it remained, a truth, evidently from God. Not that she could add anything to what Christ had done, not that she was even a martyr for his name, but such deep suffering on the part of one of his children was not insignificant to the Father.

Will I live through this? Will this child I carry live through this?

Sometime later, God held her in his lap and showed her his family photo album. She sat with the large album in front of her. It was very precious to the Father because each person was precious to him. These were his children. Each page of the album was thick, like a birthday card that has a song built in. The album was high quality but not extraordinary except that each page contained numerous circular or oval frames and in each gold encircled picture the life of one dear person continued in heaven. They were not still photos, nor were they videos but definitely moving pictures in real time. Around the edges of the page were the lives of those dearest to her, people still living here on earth, but they were somehow incomplete and she was not allowed to really look into them. This one, this one she knew was the baby she carried. God allowed her to see his shoes running and playing on the grass in the yard. He was three years old and was playing with his daddy, Peter, while she watched. Such cute shoes, such sounds of laughter, sounds of enjoyment! She was content. God had shown her that they were going to be just fine. Her relief was instant and complete.

    She chose her grandmother's frame. She wanted to see the final outcome of her grandmother's life, and so she watched her grandmother's life. But it wasn't the past, as she expected, it was showing her current events. Her grandmother continued to live, she and the many friends she entertained. Talking, visiting, laughing, they were happy and busy, peacefully going about carrying out missions to help the saints on earth, but they were in heaven. She watched for an eternity and none of her grandmother's sorrows left the slightest shadow on her present existence. It was an eternity that Caroline followed her grandmother's life, but Caroline seemed to have all of eternity to do so.

Caroline turned her attention to the circular frame of her mother's life. Again, she watched for more than a lifetime, for nothing short of an eternity, except that when she stopped looking, she knew it would go on for another eternity, and on and on. There was no weariness, no boredom, no repetitiveness. It was simply God's perfect life for her mother.

And Caroline had gained the knowledge that each person in her grandmother's life was connected in some way to all of the others. It was the same with her mother's life. Each person was a connection to God and to all of the hundreds, thousands, of other godly people coming and going in one person's life. It meant that there were a limitless number of people God used to bless each person in his or her own life. And they were all connected, continually blessing and caring for one another. This was the body of Christ, a building not built with human hands. This was the reality of what the kingdom of God is. Not what, but who. This living, interconnected, eternal life was the kingdom of God.

Peter sat by her side, holding her hand, waiting for her to wake up.

"Hello, Sunshine," he whispered with tears in his eyes.

She managed a faint smile and closed her eyes again.

"They saved the baby?" she asked.

"Yes. And you."

"I'm sorry, Peter."

"What are you sorry about?"

"The accident. If I hadn't been in such a hurry."

"It wasn't your fault. The truck ran a red light."

"But if I hadn't been in such a hurry."

"Shhhh. You were not at fault."

"They wanted to take the baby."

"But they didn't. You're both going to be fine. Can you go back to sleep now?"

She closed her eyes.

The next time she opened her eyes, the room was flooded with sunlight and filled with a variety of flower bouquets. Grandma Martha and Grandpa John came to the bedside.

"Caroline, dear." Murmured Grandma Lockwood, taking her hand.

Caroline managed another faint smile.

Grandpa explained, "Peter went home to get some sleep.

He's been here since the accident, so you're stuck with us for now."

Caroline smiled again.

"You're in ICU, you know. You had us all pretty worried. Lots of people praying," he continued, trying not to cry.

"You're going to be fine," Grandma Martha reassured her, not minding the tears running down her cheeks as she patted Caroline's hand.

Later, Peter came in and Grandma and Grandpa left so Peter's parents could come in.

"Our entire church is praying for you, dear," said his father.

After a few minutes they left so Jo and Matt could come in. They had all been praying for her.

"Everyone at seminary is praying for you."

They joked about the number of flower bouquets and told her Pastor Clay had spent the first night at the hospital, praying with Peter. Their church was praying, still.

Later, when everyone but Peter had gone, Caroline thanked the Lord for delivering her and the baby. She thanked him for all of the prayers and flowers. She thanked him for the body of Christ that was ministering to Peter and to her. *God is good.*

Caroline dangled the toy in front of baby Martha until she giggled.

"Right here, buddy!" yelled Peter after he passed the soccer ball to his son, Little John, as he was called, to distinguish him from his great-grandpa. "Kick it back to Daddy!"

Caroline sat, frozen, as she watched John's little feet on the grass of the backyard.

"Thank you, God," she whispered.

Acknowledgment

I wish to thank Malcolm Miller for interpreting and explaining to the world the stained glass windows of Chartres Cathedral. Thanks to him, the meanings of the biblical windows and sculptures, so rich in theology, have not been lost to time. Any errors regarding Chartres are mine entirely.

For More Information

For more information including a downloadable copy of the book of John devotional and updates about upcoming books, visit:

gailethulson.com

About the Author

Gaile Thulson holds an undergraduate degree from Wheaton College with double majors in Elementary Education and Biblical Archaeology, as well as a master's degree in Old Testament from Denver Seminary and two Master of Education degrees from the University of Northern Colorado. She loves learning and has enjoyed teaching a variety of subjects to a variety of ages in a variety of settings. Reading fiction is one of her favorite pastimes and, as a writer, she loves expressing her faith in Christ through the fiction genre, as well as nonfiction and poetry. Grateful for their spiritual heritage, she and her husband Mark enjoy passing the Christian values of their parents down to their own children and grandchildren.

Cup of Water Publishing

Giving a thirsty person a cup of water brings refreshment and can be lifesaving. Christ declared that such an action by his disciples would not go unrewarded. In the same way, giving a cup of spiritual water brings refreshment and can also be lifesaving. It is the mission of Cup of Water Publishing to give spiritual refreshment to any who are "thirsty" by making available material that is wholesome, Biblical, theologically sound, and edifying. Ultimately, our goal is to point the way to Jesus, the source of true spiritual water.

Made in the USA
Monee, IL
24 September 2022